Naked Danger!

Quietly Longarm returned the room key to his pocket and slid the .44-40 Colt into his hand.

He took a half step to the side so that he would not be standing directly in front of the door when it opened, then swiftly raised his right foot and kicked.

The door flew open with a crash as it was whipped around and banged into the wall. Before the door was even fully open, Longarm was in a crouch and moving forward, the big steel Colt leading the way.

The Colt wound up aimed at a wide-eyed and apparently quite startled—and quite naked—blonde . . .

TABOR EVANS

LONGARM

AND THE
CROOKED RAILMAN

A JOVE BOOK

LONGARM AND THE CROOKED RAILMAN

A Jove Book/published by arrangement with
the author

PRINTING HISTORY
Jove edition / August 1986

Copyright © 1986 by Jove Publications, Inc.
This book may not be reproduced in whole or in part,
by mimeograph or any other means, without permission.
For information address: The Berkley Publishing Group,
200 Madison Avenue, New York, N.Y. 10016.

ISBN: 0-515-08648-7

Jove Books are published by The Berkley Publishing Group,
200 Madison Avenue, New York, N.Y. 10016. The words
"A JOVE BOOK" and the "J" with sunburst are trademarks
belonging to Jove Publications, Inc.

PRINTED IN THE UNITED STATES OF AMERICA

Chapter 1

Longarm crossed his legs and leaned back in the red morocco covered chair in front of Billy Vail's desk. The U. S. marshal for the Denver district was busy pontificating about something to his clerk, Henry. Longarm did not bother listening to find out about what. Henry bobbed his head occasionally in agreement. Longarm stifled a yawn and reached for a cheroot.

"Send a copy to Parker in Fort Smith," Vail was saying. The balding, slightly plump marshal scratched the side of his nose. "And one to Austin as well, I think. No telling whose lists this boy was on."

Longarm bit off the twisted end of the cheroot and spat the residue into his fist. Anywhere else, he might have disposed of it more conveniently by letting it fall to the floor, but he knew that Vail would notice and object if he took that liberty here. The marshal was more observant, and a hell of a lot tougher, than his appearance indicated.

This had been discovered too late by a good many felons during Billy Vail's field days, when the man worked with a badge and gun instead of a clerk and pile of papers.

The lean, deeply tanned deputy thumbed a match alight and applied the flame to the end of his cheroot carefully, first allowing the tobacco to warm and then to catch. He drew the smoke into his lungs with satisfaction.

"I think that should cover everything," Vail said at last. Henry bobbed his head again and left the office, giving Longarm a wink from behind the glare off his spectacle lenses as he left the office.

"What are you doing here?" Vail asked abruptly, swiveling his chair to face Longarm across the cluttered desk surface.

"Damned if I know," Longarm answered. "You sent for me, remember?"

"I did? I did," Vail added lamely. Then he perked up. "Of course I did. Dutch was delayed in Cheyenne. That's right." He fumbled through the papers on his desk, found the one he wanted, and pulled it free. "I have a routine pickup order here. If you apply yourself to the job, you can probably handle it."

The marshal smiled a little and peered over the sheet of paper at Longarm.

"Thanks for the confidence," Longarm said dryly.

In fact, Custis Long was the district's best deputy marshal, although Longarm would never expect Billy Vail to admit that. Vail tended to give Longarm the toughest assignments to come through the office, but in this case the job would quite obviously be a piece of cake.

"Routine, you say?"

"Mmmm," Vail mused. "Let me read this again." He paused for a moment to go over the arrest order in his hands, then looked back at Longarm.

"You know Alex Gervais over in Silverton, don't you?"

Longarm nodded. "Good man," he said. Gervais was the local law there.

"Exactly," Vail agreed, "and he's done a nice piece of work here. The postmaster there, a man named Cutchell, tipped Gervais to a sudden increase in the cashing of postal money orders, and Gervais followed it very nicely. Put the cuffs on three of them, and he's transporting them up here to us for incarceration and trial."

"You want me to go down and pick them up, Billy?" It was routine indeed, Longarm thought, but necessary. The theft of postal money orders was a federal offense, falling under the Justice Department's jurisdiction and not that of the local authorities in Silverton.

"No, those three are already on the way with one of Alex's deputies," Vail said, "but there is another member of the gang still at large. The head man, in fact. He's a railroad section chief stationed at Redcloud, which is across the county line and out of Alex's jurisdiction. So I want you to go down and bring him back to join the others."

"That's it? Just arrest the man?"

Vail nodded. "That's all. We already have a signed warrant, based on the testimony of one of the gang members Gervais caught. As soon as the cuffs hit his wrists, I gather, he started to sing like the proverbial canary."

"So much for honor among thieves," Longarm said.

Vail smiled. Both men knew that such romantic notions were basically a load of bull.

"So tell me about this yahoo I'm supposed to drag in," Longarm said.

Vail turned the paper around and slid it across the desk toward Longarm. "The man's name is Walter Tomlin. As section chief on the railroad, he had access to all the cars

3

and railroad facilities, of course, including the mail car and safes. Apparently he just pilfered the money orders at his leisure and mailed them down to his pals in Silverton for them to cash in exchange for fifty percent of the take."

"Simple," Longarm said.

"And rewarding, until Gervais nabbed his friends. Incidentally, they haven't been allowed to send out any notes or letters since Alex got them. So your man should be waiting for you in Redcloud fat and dumb when you get there. He doesn't know yet that the game is up."

Longarm grunted and drew on his cheroot. He had had some vague plans for the coming weekend, but it was nothing that could not be postponed. The lady would still be around. And it had been a while since he had been able to get away from the dull work around Denver. For a change, he was not all unhappy about Vail's summons to him.

If nothing else, this little trip would give him an opportunity to get up into the high, clean air of the mountains in time to see the soft break of spring. It was a good time of year, an invigorating time, and he would much rather spend it in the high country than down here amid the coal smoke and the soot of the city.

Longarm carefully folded the arrest warrant for Walter Tomlin and slipped it into his coat pocket. "It will take me a day to get down there, say, and likely another to take the narrow gauge up to Redcloud and find our sticky-fingered section chief. Call it three days round trip, or four at the outside."

"I'll authorize you three days' expense money," Vail said. "And remember to keep your accounts in order, Custis. We aren't going to start any of this per diem nonsense. Actual expenses only."

"Right." Longarm agreed easily, if without any particular conviction, on the subject. The Justice Department's worries about paperwork were a constant, if minor, annoyance and one he tried not to burden himself with, to the sometimes major annoyance of Billy Vail and the clerical staff.

"If you have any problems, wire me," Vail added.

Longarm gave the marshal a dirty look. What problems could he possibly have with something this simple?

Longarm pulled his watch out and checked the time. He would have to stop at his rooming house for his gear, and he would want to make sure he had a fresh bottle of Maryland rye for the trip. But he saw no reason why he could not take a train west this afternoon. If he remembered correctly, he could make a connection by way of the Central City line and be in Silverton sometime late tomorrow.

"Is that it, then, Billy?"

The marshal nodded.

Longarm uncrossed his legs and flipped the stub of his cheroot, still burning, into Vail's wastebasket.

"Long!"

"I know. If I have any problems I'll wire you." He plucked his flat-crowned brown Stetson off the sideboard and got out of the office before Vail had time to squawk.

The train, mostly freight cars with a pair of passenger coaches tacked on almost as an afterthought, rumbled over Red Mountain Pass after leaving Ouray and coasted the snaky downhill stretch into Silverton.

Off to Longarm's left out of the coach windows, toward the east, he could see the jagged, snowy tip of Redcloud Peak. Somewhere below it he would find the mining camp that had been named for the mountain. Idly he wondered how the mountain had come to have that particular name. Here on the western slope of the Rockies they were many

5

miles and a fair number of mountain ranges away from the rolling, grassy plains where the Sioux chief Red Cloud hung out, so there was little likelihood that it was named after him. Probably some early mountain man or prospector had first spotted it with an evening cloud hanging over the peak, and the name had somehow stuck.

He grunted and took another look through the train windows. For damn sure there was nothing remotely similar between Red Cloud's gentle scenery and that of Redcloud Mountain.

The Sioux lands, hundreds of miles to the northeast, were a cattleman's notion of heaven, with sturdy grasses and bright wildflowers stretching across vistas greater than any man's eye or mind could rightfully comprehend.

Here, around Redcloud Mountain, a cattleman would find himself in the hell of his nightmares. Here the country stood on its ends, all up and down, gray rock and stark white snows even in the spring. And it would take a damned serious-minded cow to make a living finding the few tufts of tough, wiry grasses that were able to find soil and root-hold among the rocks and pea gravel layered over the stony base of the earth.

The trip from Denver would have been exciting for a naturalist, Longarm thought. Down in Denver, on the other side of the Rockies, it was truly coming springtime now. The early flowers were out, and the cottonwoods were coming into bud.

As the trains had carried Longarm higher, though, the soft, pale greens had fallen behind. Here even the aspen remained bare and barren, and the only indication of spring was that the snowdrifts were beginning to sag in on themselves and there was bright warmth in the strength of the afternoon sunlight.

As the train crossed Red Mountain Pass, the drifts had

still been sash-high to the coach windows. No problem. The butcherboy who sold stale sandwiches between stations had kept the stove fueled and the car pleasantly warm for the duration of the trip. Longarm had brought his sheepskin-lined coat despite the warmth of the season down in Denver; he was no pilgrim when it came to mountain travel, and he knew what the high-country spring could be like.

He yawned and took another casual look around the inside of the coach, even though he knew there was nothing worth looking at.

There was not a female in the lot of travelers with whom he was sharing accommodations. Toward the front of the car there were two separate groups of men who looked like they were probably hardrock miners. The two groups were separated, apparently, by language restrictions. One batch spoke English, the other did not. Longarm had not yet figured out just what language the foreigners did speak. Likely he never would know. Behind them were a few better-dressed men who might have been engineers or chemists. Scattered here and there were a few more who were likely drummers or peddlers.

Longarm yawned again, then straightened in his soot-grimed seat and began to perk up as he heard the squeal of protesting steel from the freight cars behind them. The brakemen were beginning to set their wheels. The rhythm of the clacking as the trucks passed over rail joints altered slightly as the drag of the brakes began to overcome the inertia of the train's weight. The cars began to slow in anticipation of the Silverton stop, and Longarm started to gather his gear together.

"You big son of a bitch!"

Longarm stiffened. The voice had come from behind. It

could have been addressed to anyone leaving the car. But still . . .

He turned slowly, ready. His left hand was encumbered by his carpetbag, McClellan saddle, and scabbarded Winchester, but the right was free and available if he had to make a reach for the big Colt that was holstered to the left of his belt buckle, butt tilted to the right for a cross-body draw.

"Long!" the same voice barked.

A drummer who had just left the passenger coach turned pale and scurried back up the metal stairs into the safety of the rail car.

Longarm completed his turn and squared off in front of the man who had spoken.

He was small, a banty rooster of a fellow, with a ferocious, heavily waxed moustache even larger and more impressive than Longarm's sweep of brown elegance.

He wore low-heeled black boots and a spotlessly clean derby hat. Between those two extremes he sported a brace of large and ugly revolvers, one rigged like Longarm's for a cross-draw, and the other, larger one dangling at his side.

He was scowling.

Longarm scowled back at him.

"You!" the little man called out in a challenging voice. Others on the platform took their cue from the drummer and tried to shuffle inconspicuously out of the way.

"By damn," the little man roared, "you're the only son of a bitch I ever seen that's uglier than I am. Welcome to Silverton." He grinned. "Welcome to God's country."

Longarm grinned back at him. "Alex, you're gonna get yourself shot someday." He stepped forward to accept Sheriff Gervais's handshake.

Both men were grinning. The people on the platform around them looked relieved.

8

Alex Gervais plucked Longarm's saddle and carpetbag away from him, insisting on carrying them. He tactfully allowed the tall deputy to retain the Winchester, then punched Longarm's shoulder. He had to reach upward a considerable distance to accomplish that.

"What's it been, Longarm? A year? Two?"

Longarm nodded. "Something like that."

"Too damn long," Gervais said.

Longarm pulled a pair of cheroots from his coat pocket, offered one to Alex, and struck a match to light both.

Alex drew deeply on the first billow of smoke from the thin cigar and sighed. "Ah. Now that's why I was glad to hear you were coming. I can always count on you to be a soft touch with a good smoke. Us poor, underpaid county yokels can't afford things like this."

"What's the matter, Alex? Are the graft and corruption letting you down lately?"

Gervais widened his eyes in a display of shock and deep hurt. "Longarm! I have to *hide* all that from the voters. Got an election coming up, you know, and I can't give them a hint of what a soft touch this job is."

"An election, huh? That explains why you got off your ass long enough to do a decent job on the money-order business."

"Decent? *Decent?* It was a marvelous job. Stupendous. And you know it." Alex chuckled. "Why, you're jealous, you son of a bitch. You couldn't have done half as good yourself, and you're jealous."

Longarm sighed loudly and theatrically. "You caught me, Alex. I'm jealous." He looked around at the squalid boomtown and the inhospitable crags that surrounded it. "I always did want to be like you, Alex. A big fish in a half-assed pond."

Gervais laughed and tugged at Longarm's sleeve.

9

"C'mon, damn you. We have time for a drink or three before Ruth has supper on the table." Happy pride came into his face and his chest swelled perceptibly as he added, "I can't give you the spare bedroom this trip, though, my friend. We've had to go an' turn it into a nursery."

"No!"

Gervais grinned and nodded. "A boy. Four months old now." The grin got bigger. "The lucky little bastard has his mother's good looks too."

"Thank goodness he doesn't take after you."

"Ain't that the truth," Gervais agreed cheerfully. "Come on, now. I have a room reserved for you, and Ruth will give us both hell if I let her roast get cold before I get you through the door."

"Roast beef, Ruth's company, and a chance to bounce your boy on my knee? Let's be moving along, little man."

Longarm followed his friend to the hotel, reflecting that at least this time he was blessed with cooperative and efficient local law on this dead easy assignment.

Yeah, he thought, this was a positive pleasure after some of the chores Billy Vail threw at him.

Why, he could almost consider the whole thing to be a springtime holiday with pay.

Chapter 2

Longarm returned to the hotel after dinner, his belly full of Ruth's good cooking, but he wanted a drink to settle the meal. Apparently there was a new rule prohibiting liquor in the Gervais household since the arrival of young Alex Junior. Longarm did not mind. Alex was a cute little bugger, all smiles and dimples and cooing. The evening had been a pleasant one, cut short at about nine o'clock, early to bed apparently being another new habit since the baby's arrival.

Longarm stopped at the desk to retrieve his room key from the clerk. He hesitated there, trying to decide between breaking into the bottle in his bag or stopping in at the adjacent bar, where they might or as easily might not have his favored Maryland distilled rye whiskey.

It was really too early to pull it in, he decided, and opted for the saloon rather than his room. He turned to his left and crossed the lobby toward the set of doors that separated the male-only drinking establishment from the open lobby area.

He tipped his hat and gave a smile to an unattended lady seated in the lobby with a newspaper in her lap.

Nice, he mused. Auburn hair piled high and severe, but its color set off nicely by the dark green velvet of her dress. Definitely pleasing features. Gray eyes. And not shy about showing them, come to think of it. She was looking straight at him over the edge of her newspaper.

Longarm could not help but feel a twinge of interest as she quite openly looked across the lobby at him.

What she was seeing was not displeasing, he hoped. He was a tall man, deep tan with brown hair, eyes the color of gunmetal, and a sweeping brown moustache. Well over six feet in height, he had broad shoulders but a horseman's lean, whipcord build, very narrow at waist and hip. He wore black stovepipe boots, brown corduroy trousers, a butternut flannel shirt with a string tie at the attached collar, a calfskin vest and a brown tweed coat, virtually his normal city wear, for the evening he had just spent with the Gervais family. He had long since come to terms with the pleasant realization that a good many women seemed to find his looks acceptable, even though his own examinations in shaving mirrors failed to explain those responses to him.

Still, he chided himself, there was no point in becoming interested in this lady now. She was likely a very prim and proper woman waiting for her large and possibly jealous husband to join her.

Her eyes met his when he touched the brim of his Stetson to her, but she did not return the expression. He looked quickly away and forgot about her as he went on into the saloon.

The saloon attached to the hotel was dark and homey, its

12

customers engaging in low conversation or drinking alone and in silence. It was not at all a rowdy hangout for miners.

The proprietor moved quickly to greet him when Longarm stepped up to the bar.

"Would it be too much to expect you to have Maryland-made rye?" Longarm asked.

The barman smiled. "Eight years in the oak or twelve?"

"You wouldn't joke with a weary traveler, would you?"

"Never," the barman said solemnly, but with a sparkle of amusement in his eyes.

"Then I'll have to ask you for the twelve and thank you," Longarm said.

The bartender found the bottle he wanted, dark and dusty, its label stained with age, and poured a generous tot. He set it in front of Longarm with a flourish.

The liquor was as mellow as summer dew. "Nectar," Longarm assured the man, "much too fine to drink in a hurry." It was like swallowing a warm cloud.

"Shall I leave the bottle, friend?"

"Please."

The barman topped off Longarm's glass, then moved down the bar to serve someone else.

Longarm turned to prop his elbows on the polished hardwood surface and raised the glass to smell the liquor, then took another taste. It was every bit as good as the first sip had been.

Silverton, Longarm thought, had much to recommend it, despite his joking with Alex Gervais. Longarm felt truly contented now.

Across the room two men in shirtsleeves were huddled deep in conversation. Longarm could not help noticing them. Aside from the fact that he was facing directly toward them, they were the only two in the place who were not wearing coats and ties. The quality of this hotel saloon was definitely a cut above the slop chutes to be found in most mining camps.

The two were seated across the table from each other, but they leaned forward so that their heads nearly touched. They seemed awfully intent.

One of them frowned, shook his head abruptly, and leaned back in his chair.

The other man's hand shot out to capture the first man by the wrist.

The first man jerked his arm free and stood, backing up with his hand darting toward his pocket.

"Here, now!" the bartender called out across the quiet room. "Take it outside if you want to fight." He hurried around the end of the bar and headed toward the two. The barman was emptyhanded except for a rag he had been using to wipe the surface of his bar.

Longarm straightened and set his glass carefully aside.

The angry man pulled a clasp knife from his pocket and, with a quick flip of his wrist, snapped it open. The steel blade gleamed wickedly in the lamplight of the room.

The barman stopped several paces away from the two, one of whom was pale now and still seated.

"Charlie," the second man said in a low warning tone.

"Shut up," Charlie snapped. "And you." He motioned toward the barman. "Get back where you belong."

The barman gave Charlie an anxious look, then glanced around the room. The place was silent now. The other customers were staring at the tableau.

Longarm moved across the room toward them. He seemed in no hurry, but within moments he was standing between the bartender and the knife-wielding customer.

"He is where he belongs," Longarm said in a slow, soft voice that probably could not have been heard five feet

14

away. "But I don't think you are, friend. Better ease off now." Longarm smiled. The expression did not reach his eyes, though, and the big .44-40 Colt was in his hand now. He held it almost casually, his body shielding it from the other patrons in the saloon. Charlie could see it, and so could Charlie's companion.

Charlie's eyes narrowed. He looked from Longarm's revolver down to the knife in his hand and then back again.

"I think maybe you should take a little walk and cool down," Longarm suggested patiently.

"Butt out," Charlie said. "This isn't your business."

"Actually, it is," Longarm said in the same soft tone. "I'm a peace officer. Just trying to keep the peace." He smiled.

Charlie grunted. It came out half a growl. Even with his knife facing Longarm's revolver he seemed reluctant to give it up. But after a moment reason prevailed, and he released the lock catch on the blade of his knife, folded the weapon, and dropped it back into his pocket.

"Thank you," Longarm said.

Charlie snarled something that Longarm did not catch, pivoted, and hurried out of the bar toward the hotel lobby. His companion looked relieved. He pulled a handkerchief from his back pocket and used it to mop his forehead, then gratefully tossed down the drink that was on the table in front of him.

"Thanks, neighbor," the barman said with heartfelt sincerity.

"No problem," Longarm assured him.

"That bottle is on me, friend. Your money's no good in here tonight."

"You don't have to do that," Longarm said.

"Don't have to, maybe, but that's the way it is."

"Then it's my turn to thank you."

15

"You're really a peace officer?"

"Uh-huh. Federal, though. I didn't think there was much point in going into questions of jurisdiction with your customer."

The bartender cooled his face with a damp bar rag and gave Longarm a weak grin. Charlie's companion swallowed off the last of his drink and left, heading out the same way his friend had gone.

Longarm returned to the bar and another drink of the excellent rye whiskey. The incident seemed over and done with, and he quickly forgot about it.

Longarm made his way up to his second-floor room, the rye a warm glow in his stomach. He reached into his pocket for his key as he turned the corner of the corridor toward his room, and stopped short.

"Hello."

The lovely auburn-haired woman in green was bent over the lock of the room next to his. She had an uncooperative key in her gloved hand and looked to be close to tears.

"May I help you, ma'am?"

"What . . . ? Oh." She gave him a look of vast relief. "Thank you, sir. I can't seem to make this awful key open the door, and I just . . ." She fought back a sob. "Here." She thrust the key toward him.

"I'll see what I can do, ma'am," he said pleasantly.

Longarm fit the stem of the key into the lock easily, but the lady was right; there was something wrong with it. No matter how he tried to twist and turn it, the tumblers would not turn. He rattled the knob and tried again with no more success than he had had the first time.

In a cheaper hotel it would have been almost as quick to pick the lock as to use a key, but the Silverton Arms had selected quality locks for their guests' protection. He frankly was not all that sure he would be able to get into one of these rooms without a proper key.

"Oh, dear," the lady wailed softly. "I just don't know what to do."

"It's all right, ma'am," he soothed her. "If nothing else, I can go down and get the clerk."

She still looked troubled.

"Is there anyone inside that you don't want to waken?"

She looked at him and blinked. "No, I am . . . traveling alone, sir." She sighed and looked unhappy. "My family told me I should have a companion, but I did *so* want to prove my independence. And now look what happens, the very first thing, practically. Oh, my."

Her eyes were very large, very gray. They were brimming with the unshed tears of frustration and perhaps of other emotions he did not know.

"Don't worry, ma'am. It isn't really all that serious. Honestly." He gave her a smile of reassurance and tried they key again, still without success.

He pulled the key from the stubborn lock and said, "I'll take this down to the room clerk. It won't take but a moment."

"Thank you, sir," she said.

He had not gone more than a few paces down the corridor when he glanced down, then stopped and began to laugh.

"Yes?"

"I think I found your problem, miss."

"What?"

"You misread the room number. See?" He held the key out for her to examine. Etched on the side of it was the number 18 in a fancy Florentine-script numeral. The door she had been trying to open was room number 28.

"Oh, my." Her eyes became even wider, and her hand

flew up to cover her pretty mouth. "You must think me a terrible dunce." She seemed to be on the verge of tears again.

"Of course not. It's a mistake anyone could make. You just took a wrong turn somewhere. May I help you find the right door?"

"I hate to be a bother, but would you, please?"

"Of course." Still with the lady's key in his possession, Longarm led her back the way he had just come and down the other branching corridor to room number 18.

He inserted the key into the lock, turned it and the door opened easily to his touch. "There you are, ma'am." Longarm touched the brim of his hat, stepped away from the open door, and held the key out to her.

The lady blushed. "I feel a perfect fool about this, sir," she said shyly. "But you have been quite the gallant gentleman. However can I express my thanks?"

"You already have, ma'am." He smiled. He was still holding the key out toward her, but she made no move to take it.

Instead, curiously, her eyes lowered, raised, lowered again coyly. A slight blush colored her cheeks. This time when she raised her eyes again they locked on his, then slowly and quite shockingly drifted down until he would almost have sworn that she was peering at a point just south of his belt buckle.

He felt a perfectly normal stir of interest at the presumed inspection, a male swelling in the neighborhood toward which she seemed to be looking. And this time he was positive about what she was looking at, because her eyes widened.

Her lips parted slightly, and the pink tip of her tongue appeared to circle and moisten her full, ripe lips.

"Would you care to come inside, sir?" The words were

proper enough, or nearly so, but there was a distinct husky catch in her throat as she said them. He thought she had begun to breathe a little harder, a little quicker. The swell of interest at his groin grew insistently.

"If you are . . ."

"Please?" She licked her lips again. She was still looking at the bulge behind his trouser buttons.

It would have been ungallant to refuse the lady's invitation. Longarm nodded and followed her inside the hotel room.

The room was very much like his own, small but impeccably clean and tastefully furnished. She held the door open while Longarm found and lighted the bedside lamp. He would have lighted the pair of wall lamps also, but the lady shook her head to tell him not to, then closed and carefully locked the door.

Longarm was having a certain amount of difficulty believing his good fortune of the evening.

The lady's manner changed once the door lock was set. She no longer looked or acted nearly so shy as he had first thought. Now she very openly assessed his lean, muscled frame and the finely chiseled features of his face.

She smiled at him, neither shy nor coy this time but blatantly bold about it, and took the few steps necessary to stand in front of him.

She flicked an imaginary speck of lint from his lapel, and her hand lingered there. She pressed her palm against his chest and ran her hand down his belly, then back up as she caressed his neck and jaw.

"You are a terribly handsome gentleman," she said. Her voice was low and throaty.

What the hell? The offer could not have been any plainer. He wrapped his arms around her and pulled her to him.

19

She came to him willingly and fitted herself against him with a fluid grace. There seemed to be no weight to her despite the soft curves and contours of her body, and her breath had the taste of mint.

Longarm thought about that for half a second or so and decided that he did indeed enjoy the flavor of mint.

Her tongue flickered into his mouth, probing deeply while she kissed him with a growing hunger. She canted her hips forward to grind against his erection. He had not realized until then just how tall she was. Her body fit his to perfection.

When finally she pulled away from him it was to unpin her hair and send it tumbling down over her shoulders, with a catlike smile.

Then, slowly, her eyes fixed on his, she began to unfasten the long line of tiny buttons that ran from the throat to the waist of her emerald dress.

Longarm swallowed and began to strip away his own clothing.

Her body had the sleek appeal of a mountain cat, long and graceful and gloriously beautiful. Her breasts were full and quite firm, tipped with pale, erect nipples. Her waist was narrow over a delicious swell of rounded hip and slender, almost muscular thighs. Her ankles were perhaps a trifle thick, and her feet knobby, but Longarm was not particularly interested in criticisms at the moment.

Her belly was flat and taut. The curling bush of pubic hair was a medium brown rather than auburn like the hair on her head, which was the crowning glory of all that silken splendor. Long and glossy and rich, it cascaded tantalizingly down over the upthrust of her breasts, swinging and shimmering in the lamplight as she moved.

She seemed to be fully aware of the effect she had on him. She posed before him, turned, posed again. All the while that faint smile remained on her lips, challenging, almost mocking.

Longarm finished stripping. He kicked his balbriggans aside and hung the holstered Colt over the bedpost, then crossed the room to her.

She raised her face to him, lips parted and wet. Instead of kissing her, as she obviously expected, Longarm bent to scoop her up in his arms and carry her without effort to the bed.

She shivered with apparent pleasure and nuzzled into his neck, the wet heat of her tongue playing over his flesh there.

"Slowly," she whispered. "Take your time, dear. We aren't in any hurry."

"The hell we aren't," Longarm mumbled. "We can take our time the *second* time."

He tumbled her onto the bed. She opened her mouth, perhaps to protest, but he covered her mouth with his and rolled on top of her.

She tried to squeeze her thighs together, but he was already kneeling between her legs. He lowered himself onto her and into her. Her eyes went wide as he thrust himself deep inside her, and she pressed herself up to meet his thrust.

Longarm plunged into her, filling her body, feeling her respond to his length and the demands of his desire.

Her arms crept around his back to lock behind him, and she raised her legs to urge him deeper.

She began to pump and buck beneath him, hard, fast, making small mewling sounds of effort and concentration with every upward stroke.

Longarm responded in kind, setting the pace for her and stepping it up.

She began to moan and sob, biting at her underlip and

kneading his back with strong fingers. Her responses rose to meet his, and within little more than a minute he could feel the shuddering, clenching convulsions as she began to spill over into a climax. He stiffened and made one last powerful lunge into her as the spasms wracked him. He was dimly aware that she had her teeth set in the flesh of his shoulder. At the moment he did not really care.

Spent and momentarily limp, he responded to her prodding and rolled away from her onto the side of the bed next to the wall.

She gave him an odd, unfathomable look and swung her lovely legs off the edge of the bed. She seemed a bit shaken, he thought, although he could not imagine why. He did not have to ask silly questions to know that he had damn well satisfied her. After all, he had been there. He knew very well what she had been feeling during those last moments.

He smiled. They could take it slow and easy the next time, just the way she wanted it. He was more than willing.

Longarm heard a faint scrape of metal against metal and looked toward the door.

The woman moved with surprising speed.

Her hand darted toward the bedpost. She snatched up the gunbelt he had hung there.

Longarm lunged for her, but he was too late. She was already moving, slipping quickly toward the far side of the room with his Colt, while he sprawled naked, belly down, on the rumpled bed.

The carefully locked hotel-room door swung wide, and a grinning Charlie stepped inside the room to join them.

22

Chapter 3

"You bastard."

For a moment Longarm was not sure which of them she was speaking to. It turned out she was talking to Charlie.

"You certainly took your time about getting here, you bastard," she went on.

Longarm was not really paying a whole hell of a lot of attention to the lady. On second thought, he had to conclude that she really was no lady.

The woman dropped his gunbelt onto the bureau against the far wall and made a halfhearted attempt to cover herself, draping one forearm across her breasts and more or less covering her pubis with the splayed fingers of her other hand.

It was really good old Charlie Longarm was watching, however.

No knife this time. Now Charlie was carrying a revolver. It was a small nickel-plated popgun of some breaktop variety, probably a Smith & Wesson.

The caliber was not large, Longarm noted. Likely a .32. Nothing like the stopping power of a .44-40 or a .45. Nothing to scoff at, either. Longarm had seen a fair number of dead bodies that got that way through the efforts of pipsqueak bullets placed where they had to be.

And a thin layer of goosebumped hide was scant protection from .32 caliber lead slugs.

Funny. He hadn't noticed the hotel room being so damned chilly before now.

Charlie, still grinning and holding the little Smith like he knew what to do with it, stepped inside the room and closed the door behind him. Longarm was not particularly encouraged to hear the distinctive snick of the lockbolt being closed.

Come to think of it, Longarm was not particularly pleased to realize now that Charlie was not making loud and angry noises.

The set-up was almost classic: irate husband; unfaithful wife caught in bed with a passing stranger; pay up or suffer loss of reputation and some unpleasant punctures of the flesh. There were teams of confidence artists who made a mighty good living just that way.

But if that was what they had in mind tonight, the script had gone awry somewhere. If that was what they had in mind—and the woman's complaint about Charlie being late would certainly hint that it was, or had been—then why was Charlie grinning instead of threatening?

Longarm had the unpleasant feeling that this time good old Charlie was going to extract revenge from his victim rather than cash.

Longarm eyed first the Smith & Wesson, then Charlie, and finally the woman. One of her nipples was exposed

24

again, but it did not look quite as interesting to him now as it had just a minute or so earlier.

Charlie leaned against the locked door and folded his arms. The grin on his lean face looked smug, Longarm decided. Apparently the cat wanted to toy with the mouse for a while now that the mouse seemed to be safely backed into a corner.

Longarm sighed and sat up. He shifted to the side of the bed and sat there, making no effort to cover himself. He tried not to allow any tension to show in his expression.

Longarm sighed again, loud enough for Charlie to hear, and said, "I expect I know what you want. So all right, you got me. The money's in my wallet."

He reached down to the floor for the coat he had discarded there and plucked both his wallet and a cheroot from the inside pocket. He tossed the wallet to Charlie and stuck the tip of the cheroot between his teeth.

Charlie ignored the thrown wallet. The thick fold of leather and papers struck his left wrist and fell to the floor unheeded.

There was no doubt in Longarm's mind now that Charlie intended to kill him. The son of a bitch had to be half crazy to be so riled over a simple dustup down in the saloon.

That grin never wavered. And now Charlie was rubbing the ball of his thumb back and forth over the hammer spur on the little revolver. He was getting close to it.

"Pick it up, honey. My gosh!" The woman started across the room toward Charlie and the fallen wallet.

Casually, in no hurry whatsoever, Longarm bit off the tip of his cheroot, spat out the speck of tobacco, and returned the cigar to his teeth.

He leaned forward and picked up his vest from the pile

25

of clothing at his feet. With thumb and forefinger he removed the watch and chain he had stuffed into the fob pocket earlier and dipped back into the pocket.

"You don't think we ought to talk about this, Charlie?" he asked.

The woman passed in front of Charlie to bend and retrieve the wallet. It was clear enough where her interest lay. Charlie's too, for that matter. He took a step to the side, and his gun hand slowly began to rise, pointing toward his naked and presumably defenseless victim.

Longarm would have preferred some other way to handle this, but his choices seemed to be limited. He certainly did not intend to sit where he was and allow Charlie to put half a dozen .32-caliber holes in his chest.

Longarm pulled out the little brass derringer that was clipped to the end of his watch chain in the place where a fob would ordinarily ride.

Charlie must have seen the glint of metal in Longarm's hand. He bellowed a protest and triggered a shot in quick but unaimed reaction.

The little gun sounded large in the confinement of the hotel room. The stink of its burnt powder filled the place, but the bullet plunked harmlessly into the wall behind and far wide of the man's intended victim.

Frantic, Charlie tried to cock the Smith again.

Longarm took his time about aiming. Fast noises never hurt anyone.

"Drop it," Longarm barked. The order was more or less expected of him, but Longarm had no hope that Charlie would heed it. Likely the poor fool never so much as heard it. He kept on trying to get off a second shot.

Even before the last sound had left his lips, Longarm triggered the derringer.

The tiny pistol, with so little weight to work against the recoil and a butt so small he could only grip it with two fingers, roared like a cannon inside the room. The recoil twisted the little brass weapon cruelly. But its thoroughly man-sized slug flew true.

The stubby chunk of lead smashed onto, into, and through Charlie's breastbone, within two inches of Longarm's point of aim, and exited rather messily just to the right of Charlie's spine, taking a large quantity of tissue and bone with it in its passage.

Charlie was no longer interested in shooting anyone, or in anything else, for that matter.

His expression changed from wicked grin to pale disbelief, and he stared down with some horror at the bright red stain spreading slowly over his shirtfront.

By that time, although he might not have realized it, he was no longer standing on his feet. His knees had given out and he had slid down the wall into a sitting position with his functionless legs folded under him.

Charlie coughed once, softly, and a scarlet bubble formed at his lips. His eyes glazed, and he was gone.

The woman—Longarm realized only then that he had never gotten her name—seemed not to understand what had happened. She looked at Longarm, then at the dead Charlie, back and forth between them.

Finally she dropped to her knees, forgetting now to try to cover herself, and shook and prodded Charlie in a vain attempt to bring life back into his corpse.

Instinct kept her priorities in order, though. She still had Longarm's wallet clutched in her hand.

Longarm recovered his gunbelt first, then his coat. He found a match in the coat pocket and used it to light the cheroot that was still clamped between his teeth. The smoke was welcome. Another drink of that twelve-year-old rye downstairs would be even more so, but there would be time enough for that later.

He had time to pull his clothes on before someone out in the hallway got up nerve enough to knock on the door. He had been hearing the voices for several minutes now.

Longarm settled his Stetson in place, reloaded the derringer, and returned it to his vest pocket. He looked down at the naked woman still kneeling beside her dead lover.

He shrugged. If she did not think to put clothes on, it was really no business of his. He did, however, bend to her long enough to tug his wallet from her stiff fingers and return it to his coat pocket. She resisted only for a moment. Then he unlocked the door and pulled it open.

"Everything's under control now," he said to the worried-looking men who had gathered in the hall. "But one of you probably should run and fetch the night deputy. He'll want to make out some reports and bring the undertaker in."

By then no one was really paying much attention to what the fully dressed and obviously unharmed deputy was telling them. Everyone was crowding around to the right of the doorway, trying to get a peek at the naked woman who was kneeling beside the body.

Longarm ambled into the county sheriff's office shortly after eight o'clock, replete from a breakfast of fried pork steaks and eggs with all the appropriate trimmings. He felt almost sinfully lazy to be getting such a late start, but there would have been no point in getting around earlier in the morning. The narrow-gauge train up to Redcloud would not pull out until 11:10, so he had time to kill.

Alex Gervais was behind his desk with his feet propped

up on an open drawer. He looked like he had already been at work for some time.

"Morning, Alex."

Gervais looked at him and tried to hide a smile of welcome. "You son of a bitch. You're not only ugly, you make a lot of work for better men."

"That business last night?"

"Uh-huh. I'll be filling out papers for a week and a half. I suppose you'll want the credit for arresting Mrs. Cutler and the brother?"

Longarm raised an eyebrow. He had slept through the routine investigation work that would have taken place after Alex's night man came into the picture, so most of this was news to him. "Alex," he said, "I don't even know who you're talking about. I never got a single name last night except Charlie's, and I never heard a last name for him."

Gervais grunted and motioned Longarm toward the coffee pot. "Make yourself useful while you're over there. Pour me a refill too."

"All right."

"The dead man . . ." Gervais pulled a sheet of paper closer and checked it to be sure of the facts his deputy had written down. "The dead man was Charles Hubert Cutler. The woman was his lawful wife, all right, name of Sarabeth Cutler. And the other man, the one you would've seen in the bar earlier, was Cutler's brother Troy."

"A family affair," Longarm observed.

"Uh-huh. And you were right about their game. A badger variation. Troy would be the set-up man, making like he was cutting in on his brother's wife. That's so the mark would know she wasn't exactly your everyday church social type of woman. Then she'd pretend to have a fall-

29

ing-out with her lover and turn to the mark for comfort. About the time the mark was ready to jump in the saddle, your friend Charlie would come busting in with his little gun drawn, and it was pay up or suffer the consequences. They made sure they traveled with a marriage certificate right handy. I haven't checked that out yet, but I don't see any reason to believe it isn't genuine, if it makes any difference."

Longarm shook his head.

"The argument Charlie and Troy got into earlier, the one you saw down in the bar, had to do with Charlie thinking the woman was holding out some of the money, which I gather she was. She was building a nest egg of her own so she could pull out on them. Charlie wanted to beat her to teach her some manners, and Troy objected." Gervais grinned. "It seems like Troy really *was* her lover. Head over heels for her. He didn't want to see her hurt. And Sarabeth, aside from being married to the one brother and having the other one on the side, was having a fling with another fellow back in Kansas City. This other one's the reason she wanted to put a stake together and get away from the Cutler brothers."

"I hope you've got all this written down," Longarm said, "because it's a lot to try to keep straight. They must have turned into a talkative pair after your man hauled them in."

Gervais grinned. "We took them off into two separate rooms and played one against the other. You know how that can work when each of them gets anxious to point fingers at the other one. That's how it worked out last night. By the way, and the reason I brought all this up, Longarm, there are Wanted posters out on all three of them. There's no telling how much could be involved from how many different places, but so far I know about

30

rewards on them offered by embarrassed folks in St. Louis and New Orleans and Ogallala. There may be others too. I expect you'd be entitled to the reward money."

Longarm shook his head. "I can't take any of it, Alex. Rules. What you ought to do is put in for it yourself. Call it a present from me to Alex Junior."

"Are you sure you want to do that, Longarm? I could put in for it in my name and pass the money along to you."

"You can't change the game just by changing the name, Alex. I couldn't do it, and I don't expect either one of us would have any use for me if I agreed to it. No, you just take that and save it for Alex Junior."

Gervais gave him a smile that was as much smirk as anything else. "There was one thing I couldn't quite get a handle on last night, Longarm."

"Mmmm?"

"That's what happened between you and Mrs. Cutler before Charlie showed up."

Longarm grinned but shook his head. That was one he did not want to answer.

Gervais laughed. "Maybe I can guess at it anyway. Because that woman *sure* don't have any use for Deputy Custis Long."

Longarm was not sure but what he should feel a bit peeved about that. After all, he might have shot the woman's husband, but she had been wanting to dump Charlie anyway. And until old Charlie showed up at the damned door he had heard no complaints from her.

Fickle damned female, he thought.

He stood and set his coffee cup aside. "You don't need me for anything, do you, since I'm not taking the credit for those birds?"

Gervais shook his head.

"Then I'll go back to the hotel and get my gear together.

31

If I miss that train today, Billy'll jump all over me about it."

"I'll save you a cell to put Tomlin in when you get back here tomorrow night. I don't think you'll have any problems with him. I'd offer to go along with you, but the sheriff up there and I, we don't get along so well."

Longarm raised an eyebrow, but Alex Gervais did not seem inclined to explain any further, and Longarm did not want to press him about it.

"Look for me on the downhaul tomorrow," Longarm said, "with Mr. Tomlin in tow."

Gervais grinned. "Tomorrow, damn you, you'll have to get up when the working folk do. It's a four-hour run coming down the mountain, and the down train pulls out at six o'clock sharp."

Longarm grimaced.

"That's right," Gervais said happily. "You can't lay abed like the leisure class tomorrow."

The two men shook hands and said their goodbyes, and Longarm headed back toward the hotel to collect his gear.

Chapter 4

Gervais had said the downhaul was a four-hour trip, but the uphill run to Redcloud was a slow and grinding five-and-a-half-hour pull for a pair of narrow-gauge steam engines.

The country through which the tracks climbed became more and more spectacular—and more and more vertical to either side of the tracks—the farther they got from Silverton. Longarm marveled at the fact that the engineers had been able to find grades leading deeper into the mountains that a train could negotiate. To either side of him the sharp, rising masses of rock were such that he was not sure a goat could have found a suitable path.

Yet at some time in the recent past men and mules had invaded this rugged, inhospitable land, carrying with them sacks of beans and rock hammers. One or more of them had been persistent enough and lucky enough to have struck his lode, and the town of Redcloud had come into being.

Incredible, Longarm thought.

And now there was even the twin track of the rails leading high into the crags to haul out the ores that were mined
there. Truly incredible.

Within half an hour of leaving the tiny depot at Silverton they were passing through the past winter's snowdrifts
again, scattered at first and then almost constant on either
side of the laboring train.

At first, at the lower elevations, the slopes above the
tracks had been white as well, packed with old snow, the
top of the fields glazed and shiny in the midday sunlight,
the snowpack gently slumping lower and melting from
beneath the hard, icy surface in the warmth of the spring
sun.

Later, as the train reached ever higher elevations, the
slopes above the tracks became barren again, showing gray
rock and scattered gravel instead of the white snowpack.

That made no sense until Longarm realized that now
they were passing through terrain so steep on either side
that even in the depths of winter the slopes were too steep
to hold a pack of fresh snow. Snow that fell there would
accumulate only briefly before falling away in slides of
enormous power and strength. Avalanches. That, he realized, was why there were so few trees growing above the
tracks here. Any vegetation that tried to establish itself on
those steep mountainsides would be quickly swept away by
the frequent slides.

The train and tracks passed often through stoutly timbered snowsheds, spiked with steel into the solid granite of
the mountainsides and angled so that the avalanches would
pour over the tracks without ripping out the roadbed.

The avalanches, too, would be the reason the roadbed
so often clung to the sides of the slick rock, well above the
gorge bottoms where an inexperienced traveler likely

34

would have thought the going to be better. Because during much of the year those bottoms would be buried deep with snow, and no shed or shelter built by mere man would have been able to withstand the weight of the winter snows.

Thank goodness this job didn't break till the springtime, Longarm thought to himself at one point as the narrow-gauge train lumbered over a short span of trestle and plunged into one of the frequent tunnels that knifed through protruding fingers of solid stone. Redcloud would not be the place for a winter resort.

Eventually the tracks snaked painfully into the long, narrow gorge where the town of Redcloud lay, its namesake mountain a white and jagged sentinel above it.

He could see from the coach windows that the town was a clutch of weather-grayed buildings set along the banks of the stream that had carved the gorge. The gorge—or canyon, gulch, or hollow, depending on where the speaker hailed from in his youth—ran roughly northeast to southwest, deep and narrow amid the surrounding mountains.

On the sharp slopes to either side he could see tunnel openings, zigzag foot or mule paths climbing to them and the telltale pale paths of tailings dumps flowing down the mountainsides from the mouths of the more prosperous and active of the mine shafts.

There seemed to be no smelter or even stamp mill in the town, which probably accounted for the necessity of the railroad. The metal-laden ores would have to be sorted, crushed, and hauled down to Silverton's mills for processing.

That, Longarm realized, was probably much of the reason why a venal and greedy railroad boss up here would have turned to preying on postal money orders instead of precious metal shipments. Any son of a bitch fool enough to steal a load of unmilled ore was welcome to the troubles he was bringing on himself; forty dollars to the ton was good pay from a hardrock mine.

The train pulled to a stop at the Redcloud depot, a covered platform with a shack built at one end of it for railroad employees only, and no passenger accommodations. Longarm buttoned his sheepskin coat before stepping out into the crisp, thin air. Springtime might have been in full flower down in the flatlands, but Redcloud somehow had failed to get that message. At this elevation the atmosphere was still crisp and biting, and there was no hint of bud-green—or even so much as green paint—anywhere that Longarm could see.

Longarm reached for a cheroot and stood on the platform for a moment to get his bearings. He needed to find a hotel, the jail, and Walter Tomlin, in that order. Then tomorrow he could get back down to Silverton and spring-time. He lighted the cheroot, grunted once softly to himself, then headed down the street toward a hand-lettered sign on a two-story building that advertised itself as a hotel.

"Is the sheriff in?" Longarm hesitated just inside the doorway. He was not particularly impressed by what he saw. The sheriff's office and jail were a single room with log walls on the sides and front, the three-sided structure backed up against bare rock at the rear. The logs had once been chinked with mud, but now the material was dried out and crumbling, so the evening breeze could come whistling through almost unchecked. It would have been a hell of a place in the winter, he thought.

The jail portion of the room was at the rear of the building. It consisted of a number of iron eyebolts driven and/or cemented into the back wall of solid granite. Chains and ankle shackles lay on the granite floor. At the moment there were no prisoners attached to them. Longarm gave the arrangement a disbelieving look. He damn sure would not want to be thrown into Redcloud's pokey.

The only occupant of the place right now was a rheumy-eyed old bastard who had more gray than dark in his hair and the stubble of his beard. The old fellow showed a few stubs of yellowed teeth in a face that was seamed and filthy with age and inattention. The man gave off a sour odor of stale whiskey that seemed to come from his pores as well as his clothes. He was obviously a rummy and, judging from the loose skin that hung on his scrawny frame, he had progressed to the stage where nearly all of his meals came out of a bottle. He wore bib overalls, a faded and stained union suit, and clodhopper shoes, but no socks or shirt. He was bareheaded, and what little hair he had left was a tangle of grease.

"I'm the sherf," the rummy said. He said it with a certain amount of dignity that was spoiled by the sour belch that escaped from him immediately afterward.

"Sheriff Maxwell? Evan Maxwell?" Longarm hoped this man was playing a joke on him.

"That's right," the sheriff said, again with that hint of now-lost dignity in his voice. He fumbled for a pocket, had some difficulty locating it, then pulled out a tarnished badge to display. "Sherf Evan Maxwell." He belched again and wiped his mouth with the back of his hand.

If the man had a firearm, long or short or any kind at all, Longarm could not see it. He had the uncharitable thought that if Sheriff Evan Maxwell had owned a weapon at some time in the past he would by now have swapped the thing for a drink.

Longarm tried to keep his disapproval out of his expression. He could not help feeling it, but he honestly tried to avoid showing it. He was not sure whether he was success-

37

ful, but he gave it his best efforts.

"Deputy United States Marshal Custis Long, Sheriff," he announced. "I have an arrest warrant for one of your citizens, authorized by a judge from the Denver district, United States Justice Department. The normal procedure is for me to pay you the courtesy of informing you that I am operating within your jurisdiction."

"Course it is," Maxwell said. The sheriff blinked twice, swayed, and sat quickly back into the chair behind his desk. He looked like he had a choice between sitting again or falling down.

The man's eyes wandered aimlessly around the small room for a moment, then regained their focus and returned to Longarm. "'Scuse me an' my manners. Have a seat, Deppity. Lang, you said?"

"Long," Longarm corrected. "Custis Long. Out of Marshal William Vail's office." He looked quickly around the room. Maxwell had invited him to sit, but there was no chair or stool, not even a box for him to sit on. Maxwell seemed not to notice the lack.

"Fine. Fine, Deppity," Maxwell said. The voice started strong, with a ghostly echo of past authority, then weakened into a loose-lipped whisper. "An' you want me t' serve this here . . ." He paused to cover his mouth and belched loudly. "This warrant?" he continued.

"No," Longarm said quickly. "No, I just wanted you to know that a federal officer was here."

Maxwell smiled brightly, almost sweetly. It made him look younger. He bobbed his head in happy understanding.

It occurred to Longarm that he had been guessing the sheriff's age to be in his fifties or sixties, but the man might well have been twenty years off what Longarm would have first guessed. He did not want to ask.

"Fine," the sheriff said.

"Yes . . . well . . . thank you."

Longarm turned and got the hell out of there. It was . . . he had to think about it for a moment before he could put a tag to it . . . it was embarrassing to remain in that office.

Longarm wondered what kind of man Sheriff Evan Maxwell might once have been, and what had brought him to this state with a peace officer's badge still in his pocket.

He shuddered, unsure of whether to feel sympathy for the man or to be annoyed at him.

This, he hoped, was no augury of his own future in the service of the law. If he ever once came to suspect that, that would be the day he packed it in. He hurried back toward his shabby hotel room.

Finding Walter Tomlin was no trouble at all. After supper, Longarm walked over to the railroad depot. A plump clerk was doing some late paperwork and a telegrapher was still on duty. The train Longarm had come up on had already pulled out again for the night freight run back to Silverton and its scheduled return before morning.

Longarm idly noted as he returned to the depot that even though Redcloud was an end-of-track for the little narrow-gauge rail line, there was no roundhouse here, nor even much of an equipment shed to handle the maintenance work. Apparently the two small engines pulled forward on the uphill run and backed all the way to Silverton on the twice-daily downhauls. Not a classy arrangement, but cheap, and just as efficient as the way one of the bigger lines would have done the job.

"Hello," Longarm greeted the clerk as he stepped into the small shelter at the end of the depot platform. The two railroad employees had a fire going in the potbelly stove against the back wall. Its warmth felt good. Damned if the air here didn't have the same feel to it in April that

39

Longarm would have expected from a Denver January. He turned the collar of his sheepskin coat back down where it belonged and removed his gloves. One of these men, after all, might well be Tomlin.

"The next train down won't go till morning," the clerk said. "An' you can't wait here for it. We got no passenger accommodations." The room was warm, but the man's voice was not. He sounded bored.

"I'm looking for Walt Tomlin," Longarm said.

"What d'you want him for?" The clerk did not sound particularly suspicious about it, merely bored. The telegrapher had his nose buried in a magazine and was ignoring the conversation.

"A friend asked me to look him up," Longarm said. That was not a lie. Most of the time he did consider Billy Vail to be a friend as well as a boss.

The clerk grunted and used the heels of both hands to sweep a stack of papers into a neatly squared pile.

"I asked . . ." Longarm began again, willing to become testy about it if the clerk insisted.

"I know, damn it, I know. Give me a minute here." The clerk finished pushing his paperwork into stacks, piled several of them together, and put the whole mess into a desk drawer. He turned his head to look back toward the telegrapher. "I'm leaving it to you, Frank. You know where to find me if you need anything." He looked back to Longarm. "I'm going over there now, mister, so I expect you can tag along if you want."

Longarm nodded and opened his mouth intending to thank the man. He stopped, though, and gave the telegrapher silence when the telegraph key began to clatter. The clerk stopped too, in the middle of fetching his coat and hat from a rack against the wall.

The telegrapher picked up a sharpened pencil and

almost absentmindedly began to jot down the stream of letters that was chittering in over the wire. Longarm eavesdropped on the routine message. It would have been difficult for him not to have read it even if there had been some reason for him to try. The fist on the distant sending key was quick but crisp, and the message letters came through in a smooth, fluid flow. When the message was in, the Redcloud operator dropped his pencil, grunted once, and returned to his reading.

"What was that about?" the clerk asked. Apparently he had not picked up any ability to read the staccato clicketyclack of the electrified keys.

"Nothing much," the operator said. "Snow down in Silverton. Don't know why they'd bother us with that."

"Rules," the clerk said, pulling on his coat and buttoning himself into it. "Besides, if they're getting it down there now we'll be getting some up here in a few hours."

"I suppose," the telegraph operator muttered. He was still giving his attention to the magazine in front of him.

"Let me know if they come through with any train orders, Frank."

"I will," the operator said without looking up.

"You ready, mister?" the clerk asked.

Longarm nodded, and the clerk led him back out into the night. The chill in the air felt even deeper to him now, although probably that was only a result of having been inside with the heat pouring out of the potbelly. He turned the collar of his coat up again.

"Are you a drinking man, mister?" the clerk asked abruptly. Longarm was rather taken aback by the unexpected question. "The reason I asked, mister, is that Walt is a good ol' boy, if you know what I mean. Like to have his friends around in the evenings an' do some drinking. An' I don't think Walt's ever met a man that wasn't his friend."

The clerk smiled for the first time. He no longer looked bored. "Real good fella, Walt. You'll like him."

Longarm nodded and thought about the warrant that was folded and riding in his coat pocket along with the wallet and badge. The good old boy was going to get himself a surprise tonight.

They walked out onto the single street of Redcloud, a street that ran through the long, narrow town at the bottom of the long, narrow gorge high amid the mountains, and turned left.

"Unless he's needed on the road," the clerk explained, "old Walt's at home every evening about now with his door open to all the boys an' no corks in his bottles. I'll show you to him and maybe have a snort myself before I go for supper."

"I appreciate it," Longarm said.

"No problem."

They walked on through the cold night air, past the honky-tonk sounds of pianos and laughter and loud voices as the mining men of Redcloud got rid of their day's wages in the many saloons that comprised a clear majority of the Redcloud business establishments.

Saloons were not the only constant in a mining camp like this one. Longarm saw half a dozen dimly lighted places with heavy draperies over the windows and lanterns hanging outside that had red glass in their frames. A loudly whooping and bald-naked drunk reeled out the front door of one of them to shout something at the stars. A woman who was not much more dressed than he dashed outside to take him by the arm and guide him back inside. The clerk chuckled. Longarm did not.

"Just a little ways further now," the clerk said when they were past the whorehouse.

"I appreciate you going so far out of your way," Longarm said.

The clerk shrugged. "No problem. Really. I'd've been dropping in there later anyway. We most all do. Walt's a real good man to work for. Popular hereabouts."

That popularity was likely to take a serious decline once the news got around, Longarm reflected, but he said nothing about it to the clerk.

Tomlin's house was one of the last in town. It was set back from the street, thirty yards or so up the steep mountainside that enclosed and limited the growth of the camp. They had to climb a footpath and at the last a set of stone steps to reach the front porch. Tomlin had built an iron guard rail along the steeper portions of the climb. In winder that handrail would probably be a welcome protection from the ice and packed snow on the steps, particularly for tipplers on their way down from the house.

The house itself was fairly large, two stories and sturdily built with brick and milled lumber. Longarm had never thought to ask if Tomlin was a married man. It always bothered him to take a man away from his family, but it was something he had done before all too often and would have to do again, he knew. He had scant sympathy for men who had earned arrest, but he hated to cause that kind of pain for such men's innocent wives and children. He thought about asking the clerk if Tomlin was married, then decided there was no point in raising questions now.

They climbed to the front porch of Tomlin's house and the clerk led the way inside without knocking.

Half a dozen men were lounging with drinks in their hands in a front room that must have been designed as a parlor but which had been furnished like a clubroom for males only. A bar of sorts had been set up at the far end of

43

the room, and there was at least a case and a half of liquor bottles in evidence.

Walter Tomlin was not a family man, Longarm decided.

The drinkers all grinned and hollered out greetings when the clerk and Longarm appeared. They seemed a happy crowd.

"Evening, boys," the clerk said just as happily. He shed his coat and hat and tossed them onto a bench in the front hall that was already piled high with other coats and caps.

"Walt. Got a man here as wants to meet you," the clerk said.

Longarm had more or less expected the host to be the tall, handsome man who was seated at the far end of a leather-covered sofa.

Instead the man who stood, smiling and friendly, was a stocky, red-faced fellow with red cheeks and Burnside whiskers under a balding dome. Tomlin was wearing jeans and an undershirt and was sock-footed. He looked like he had already had a drink or three.

"C'mon in," Tomlin called out in an overloud voice. He grinned a welcome at Longarm.

Longarm glanced at the other smiling faces in the room and took the precaution of unbuttoning his coat before he announced himself. Walter Tomlin was a man who had friends, and there might be need of the big Colt that rode on Longarm's belt.

He debated whether to go ahead and pull it, then decided against that. Better to keep this thing as friendly as possible if he could Instead he reached for the warrant in his pocket.

"Walter Tomlin?" he asked.

"That's me," Tomlin said with a chuckle. "Dennis, bring the gentleman a drink, will you?" One of the other men rose and headed for the bar.

"No thanks," Longarm said mildly. "Mr. Tomlin, I'm Custis Long, deputy United States marshal. I have to tell you that I have a warrant here for your arrest. You're welcome to read it and to defend yourself in a court of law."

The faces in the room went blank, as did Tomlin's. Dennis stopped his movement toward the bar.

"You can't be serious," someone protested.

"Sorry," Longarm said, "but I am."

Tomlin's face sagged. He looked gray, Longarm thought, and suddenly years older. He did not ask what the charge against him was. But then, Longarm figured, he already knew what it would have to be.

"You don't have to put cuffs on me, do you?" he asked.

Longarm hesitated only for a moment. Then he shook his head. "No, not unless you make it necessary."

"Thank you," Tomlin said in a dull, hollow voice.

"You'll want to get some shoes on," Longarm suggested, "and bundle up. It's getting pretty cold outside."

Tomlin nodded.

The rest of the men in the room sat or stood in dumb silence, shocked to be suddenly seeing their friend and boss taken away by an officer of the law.

"I'd appreciate it if you'd get your things now, Mr. Tomlin," Longarm said softly. ·

Tomlin nodded again and moved toward the hallway. He walked with a peculiar, stiff-legged gait. That was not normal, Longarm knew. He had seen it often enough before. It was a matter of disbelief and shock, not of something wrong with his legs.

Longarm followed the man quietly upstairs to a boar's nest of a bedroom and waited with him while Tomlin assembled a small kit of shaving gear and soap, then took fresh clothing out of a large wardrobe and began to dress.

The men who had been drinking downstairs were still

quiet. After a few minutes Longarm heard some subdued footfalls as the men filed silently out of this house of sudden pain.

Longarm found himself wanting to apologize for the intrusion. He steeled himself against the rare impulse and waited for Tomlin to finish with his preparations for the trip to jail.

Chapter 5

They stepped out onto the porch. Longarm turned up his coat collar against the cold but did not button the coat. He wanted the freest possible access to his Colt in case one of those friends of the prisoner decided to do something foolish.

Tomlin paused there to close his coat and pull his gloves on, another luxury Longarm did not give himself. The man raised his eyes toward the sky. "Weather coming, it looks like," Tomlin observed.

"Oh?"

"Take a look."

Longarm did. Just a few minutes earlier when he had entered Tomlin's house the sky had been a field of diamond-studded black satin as the stars spread out overhead against the clear night sky. Now he could see that sprinkling of bright white only across the eastern half of the visible sky. Immediately above them was a nearly straight line of solid black, extending as far as he could see to the west. The cloudy front rolled silently from west to east, obliterating stars one after another even as Longarm watched. It was moving rapidly.

Longarm recalled that the railroad clerk had predicted weather here within a couple of hours after the report from Silverton came in over the wire. That had been half an hour ago or thereabouts. Apparently this front was moving faster than the clerk had expected.

The air was definitely much colder now than it had been, Longarm was sure. He tugged his Stetson tighter on his head and shivered.

"Cold," Tomlin observed.

"Uh-huh."

Tomlin smiled. He seemed to have come to some measure of acceptance of the situation by now, having had a little time to adjust to it. "It wouldn't hurt my feelings any if the upbound couldn't make it through, I reckon."

"Don't count on it."

Tomlin smiled again, easier this time. "We get some of our worst weather this time of year."

"I don't know that the weather-maker listens to the prayers of thieves," Longarm said.

Tomlin laughed. He stuck his hands deeper into his pockets and shrugged. "Well, Marshal, there's one thing I got to thank you for anyway. You been straight enough with me, letting me go along without the cuffs. I 'preciate that, and I'll give you my parole. My solemn word on it that I won't try and run on you."

Longarm nodded. Tomlin was giving his solemn word. That was all right as far as it went. The thing was, Longarm had no idea just how far it did go. If there had ever been a time in history when a man's spoken parole was as good as a set of steel shackles, that time had long since passed. That was one of the things Longarm had learned quite some time ago. A man who was willing to steal generally won't be bothered a whole hell of a lot by picayune offenses like lies.

Still, if the man really was willing to be cooperative, that was all to the good. Longarm was not going to reject any offers freely made and honestly kept. "Thanks," he said.

"Could I ask another favor of you, Marshal?" Tomlin asked as they started down the steep steps toward the road below.

"You can always ask. I make no promises until I hear what you want, though."

"Fair enough. What it is, Marshal, I need to let the railroad know that I'm what you might call 'temporarily unavailable.' So they can get somebody up to take my place and all that. I need to send a wire out. No need for me to sent it personal, really, but I'd like to have one of the boys come up and carry a message for me. Would that be all right?"

"Sure." Longarm could see no harm in letting this prisoner or any other put things in order before he went off to jail, especially when a prisoner was being reasonably helpful about the situation. "No reason why you shouldn't."

"Thanks," Tomlin said with obvious sincerity.

They walked together up the street, past the whorehouses and the saloons and the few other businesses of Redcloud.

At least some of the men who had been at Tomlin's had been talking already, that was plain. At least half the men they passed on the street stopped to stare as Longarm and his prisoner went by. Tomlin neither looked nor acted like a man who was in custody, yet a large percentage of the men on the street seemed to know that he was. Most of them nodded to Tomlin and muttered low words of encouragement and support to the railroad section chief. Tomlin was, or had been, a popular man in Redcloud.

Longarm ignored the hard looks he was given along the way. He knew no one here, and they did not know him. The people of the town had no reason to like or trust him, and all they knew about this deputy U. S. marshal was that he was carting off good old Walt Tomlin on some unexplained legal charges.

That was all right. Longarm had been there before. And at least for the time being no one seemed interested in getting nasty about their disapproval.

Before anything like that could happen, Longarm expected to be on the downtrain to Silverton with his prisoner in custody and nothing in store except an easy slide to Denver.

They reached the front of the jail, and Tomlin stopped in the street before it. For the first time since they had left the house, the man seemed to be uneasy.

Longarm thought about the conditions in that jail, realized what Tomlin must be thinking, and decided he could not blame the man.

Besides, Longarm did not want to spend the night in there any more than Walter Tomlin likely did, and Longarm knew better than to trust Tomlin and his friends to leave things be if the deputy was not right there to keep an eye on them. Sheriff Evan Maxwell could not be counted on for anything more important than the emptying of liquor bottles.

"Look," Longarm said, "I can't blame you for not wanting to be chained to the rock in that rathole. And you did give me your parole." Just because Custis Long did not particularly believe in the man's spoken word did not mean he was unwilling to play on it for whatever it happened to

50

be worth. "If you'd rather, Tomlin, we can go on to the hotel. I'll get them to scare up a cot to put in my room, and you can sleep on that. I'll have to cuff you to something overnight, of course, but you'll be more comfortable than in the jail."

Tomlin looked truly relieved. "Damn but you're a good man, Marshal. I appreciate that. I do."

"All right, then."

They walked on the extra half block to the hotel, and Tomlin led the way inside.

Here too they seemed to have heard already that Walter Tomlin was not a free man. The room clerk gave Tomlin a look of pity, gave Longarm a stark glare of disapproval, and then quickly sent a teenage bellboy scurrying for the requested cot along with blankets, pillows, and anything else Tomlin might want.

"There will be an extra charge for the double occupancy," the desk clerk told Longarm.

"Put it on my bill," Longarm told him.

"Damn right I will," the clerk said. "An' don't you worry, Walt. Comes the time, we'll have character witnesses for you enough to fill that courtroom." The man gave Longarm an accusing look as if daring him to object, but Longarm said nothing. Tomlin was entitled to that, just the same as any other prisoner before the bar. Whatever happened in the courtroom was none of the deputy's worry anyway. Longarm's job was simply to take Tomlin in and turn him over to the Justice Department as quietly as he reasonably could.

"Would you do me a favor, Mike?" Tomlin asked.

"Just you name it, Walt, and I'll do it."

"Send somebody to find Franklin, would you, and get him up to the room so I can talk with him. I need to send a wire down to the main office."

51

"I'll do it myself, Walt. Right now." The clerk slapped Longarm's room key down in front of him and turned to get his coat and woolen cap.

Longarm led the way upstairs and opened the room door. Tomlin went in without protest. The bellboy showed up within half a minute lugging a folding camp cot and an armload of bedding. The boy put the cot in the corner where Longarm directed and left without waiting for a tip.

"This should do," Longarm said.

There was a small radiator under the room's one window and a steampipe feeding it that came up through the floor. Longarm shifted the cot closer to the radiator and pulled his handcuffs from his pocket.

Tomlin readily moved from the bed where he had been waiting and offered Longarm his wrist. The deputy snapped one end of the cuffs on him. Tomlin himself closed the other end around the steampipe, locking himself securely in place there. He would not be going anywhere now until or unless Longarm decided he should. Not without wrenches or saws and a hell of a lot of noise, he wouldn't.

"You've been right decent about this, Tomlin," Longarm said.

"I got no quarrel with you, Marshal. Besides, you been decent to me too. It's the least I can do in return." Tomlin smiled. "An' I'd feel better if you was to call me Walt. Everybody does."

"All right. You can call me Longarm." He smiled. "Which not *quite* everybody is agreeable to."

Tomlin laughed.

"Have you had supper?" Longarm asked.

"That I have, Longarm."

"All right, but from here on out the U. S. government stands treat for your meals. Until you work through it, however that may be. I wouldn't know about that, of course, but I won't be shy about telling the judge how you've acted in custody. I can't make you any promises, but it could make some difference for you."

"Thank you, Longarm." Tomlin smiled. "I got to tell you the truth, though. I don't expect any miracles. I sure done it. I stole those money orders and shared the money with my friends, an' I've damn sure enjoyed spending my share of it on myself and my friends here. I don't try to weasel off of any of that, Longarm. I went and did what I'm accused of." Tomlin was still smiling.

Longarm could hardly believe he had heard that. It was one damned rare bird who would admit to a crime. All the prisons were always filled with innocent men, it seemed. Yet Walter Tomlin was smilingly admitting to the whole affair.

It was a little late to warn the agreeable fellow that now Longarm would be duty bound to relay that confession to the judge when the case came to trial. But damned if Longarm wouldn't have warned him if he had thought about it beforehand. Old Walt really *was* a likeable sort.

There was a knock on the door, and Longarm's hand moved a fraction of an inch or so toward the butt of his Colt. "Who is it?"

"Franklin Jewett. Walt sent for me?"

"Yeah. Come in."

Jewett turned out to be the telegraph operator Longarm had seen in the depot office a little while earlier. He came in with his hat in his hand and no weapons visible.

Jewett sat on the cot beside the manacled Tomlin, and Longarm turned away to rummage in his bag for the next day's clean underclothes and the bottle of Maryland rye that he would want to crack a little later.

Longarm found himself paying too little attention to

53

Jewett and the prisoner and reminded himself sharply not to be so trusting that he allowed himself to get into any trouble here.

After all, this was straight, routine work. But just about the time a man decided he could trust his life to some felon's good will, he was sure to have himself the kind of trouble no lawman wanted. After that Longarm paid closer attention to what the two were doing over on the other side of the small room.

There appeared to be no need for such caution, which was just exactly the way Longarm wanted it. Slow and easy would do just nicely.

A gust of wind rattled the windowframe, and Longarm looked out into the darkness. There was enough lamplight coming through nearby windows to show him that it had begun to snow now. He could hear the small, hard spicules of it ping off the glass as a rising wind drove it almost parallel to the ground.

This is a good night to stay indoors, Longarm thought.

Jewett thanked the marshal and excused himself, and Longarm went to the tiny bureau to retrieve his bottle of rye. He hoped someone would be building a fire in the boiler downstairs tonight, because there was a chill in the room.

Longarm came awake abruptly, his hand darting automatically for the butt of his Colt even before he consciously identified the sound that had wakened him.

Across the room Tomlin was still asleep, a low, fluttering mutter of snores bubbling past his slack lips.

Someone knocked on the door again, louder this time, followed by a voice. "Walt? Walt. You in there, Walt?"

Longarm sat up and shoved the big Colt back into the holster that was slung on the bedpost. He rubbed his eyes and swung his legs over the edge of the bed. Tomlin's gentle snoring hesitated, then resumed. "Who is it?" he called.

"Is that you, Walt?"

" No, damn it, this is Marshal Long."

"I need to talk to Walt."

"He's asleep. He's also in federal custody and not on duty right now. And you still haven't told me who you are." Longarm palmed the Colt again and left the bed, moving off to the side of the room in case the unidentified party out there was having thoughts about putting a bullet through the thin wood of the door into the lawman and freeing good old Walt.

"This is Franklin Jewett, Marshal, and I just got to talk to Walt."

"Just a minute."

Longarm found the bedside lamp, removed the globe, and struck a match. Flame took hold on the corner of the wick and spread across it, bathing the small room in the soft yellow glow of its light. Tomlin was coming awake finally. He stirred and groaned, then began to blink. "What is it?"

"Jewett," Longarm said. "He wants to see you."

"Sorry, Longarm." Tomlin sat up. He was still clothed from the waist up. The handcuff linking his wrist with the steam pipe had made it impossible for him to remove his undershirt or the flannel shirt he had pulled on before they left the house.

"Just a minute," Longarm called out loud enough for Jewett to hear. He padded barefoot to the door, the Colt still in his hand, and opened it.

Jewett was alone in the dim hallway. He was unarmed. He was also wrapped mighty heavily in a knee-long buffalo coat and woolen muffler. Both the coat and the muffler were crusted with melting snow, and the man's hair and exposed skin were wet with it.

"Come in," Longarm said. He leaned out to make sure the hallway was empty, then closed and relocked the door. He went back to the bed and fumbled on the nightstand for his cheroots, then picked up his watch. The Ingersoll indicated it should be nearly dawn now, although there was no hint of light outside the room's window.

"We got troubles," Jewett was telling Tomlin.

"Calm down, Franklin. What's wrong?"

"The upbound. It's overdue, Walt. And when I tried to raise Silverton to ask them about it, the wire was dead. I couldn't get anything out of it. Not a spark."

"Nothing?" Tomlin asked.

Jewett shook his head. "Not a thing."

The railroad boss looked past Jewett to Longarm, then helplessly back toward the steel manacles that bound him to the steampipe.

"Tell me about it," Longarm said. He raised the lamp and held the mouth of the globe under the tip of his cheroot to get the tobacco lighted.

"Well, Marshal, that's about it, really. The train is overdue, and the wire must be down."

"Any idea what could have caused that?" Longarm's first thought was that some of Tomlin's railroad buddies, Jewett perhaps among them, might well have done something to keep the law from carting their pal out of town.

Jewett gave Longarm a disgusted look. "Open that window over there, Marshal, an' see what you think."

Longarm pulled the curtain aside. "Oh."

He did not have to open the sash to see what the telegrapher meant. The glass was crusted solid and deep with an application of blown snow. It was one of those wet, heavy spring snows, completely unlike the dry, fine powder of the winter falls, or it would not have clung to the vertical glass surface like that.

"It's been blowing to beat hell the whole night long," Jewett said. "If the drifts get any higher it's gonna take snowshoes just to get from here to the depot. Hell, I fell down twice coming over here just now. And it don't look like it wants to let up any time soon."

Tomlin tried to stand but was brought up painfully short by the confinement of the handcuffs. He made a face and sat down on the cot again. "I got to get over there, Longarm," he said. "I got to see what's happening."

"You said the wire is down, Jewett?" Longarm asked.

"Must be. That's the only thing I can figure, anyhow."

"Then I can't see that you'd accomplish much by going over there, Walt," Longarm said. "You wouldn't be able to learn anything."

"But I have to organize a rescue crew. That upbound could be trapped somewhere on the road. You don't know the kind of slides we get around here. The crew . . . passengers . . . they could be caught somewhere in this. I have to get the boys moving."

Longarm hesitated, then shrugged. "I suppose you can be in custody there as easy as here." He got his trousers and found the key to Tomlin's cuffs. "But don't try to run on me, Walt. I take things like that real serious."

Tomlin snorted. "Run, Longarm? Comes weather like this, man, there's no place to run *to*."

Tomlin stood and rubbed at his chafed wrist where the handcuff had just been. His shoulders straightened, and he took on an air of authority. All Longarm had seen of the man before had been the easygoing partyer set on having a fine time with his chums. Now he looked serious and intent. For the first time Longarm could understand why this man had been so successful as a section chief for the rail line.

"Call up the boys, Franklin. Find Tony and Kent first. Tell them to rouse out the rest of the bunch. I want everyone to report to me at the office."

"Not to your house, Walt?"

"The office," Tomlin repeated. "Fast as they can make it, but to take time enough to wear their heaviest gear. Every man to bring two changes of wool socks and two extra pairs of gloves. Once you get Tony and Kent started, Franklin, I want you to go by Miss Emma's and have her make up box lunches for everyone. Four sandwiches apiece, dried fruit if she has any on hand, and packets of ground coffee in every box. You got that?"

Jewett nodded.

"Then beat it back to the depot. I'll meet you there. Don't wait on the lunches. I'll send someone for them."

"Right," Jewett said crisply.

Tomlin was already pulling his clothes on. "That's it for now, Franklin. Get on with it."

"Right." Jewett turned and let himself out of the room, moving quickly.

"Are you ready, Longarm?"

"I will be in a minute."

Longarm checked in his carpetbag, but he already knew what he had there and what he did not. He had left the warmth of spring back in Denver and had known enough to bring along the sheepskin coat and some gloves. But that was just about all the cold-weather gear he had brought. The woolen union suit had already been discarded for the year, and his gloves were unlined and of thin, close-fitting leather, suitable for handling a weapon while offering some protection from the cold, but certainly not for anything serious. His boots, too, were plain, unlined cavalry-style footwear, not intended for climbing through deep, wet snowdrifts.

He put on his heaviest shirt and buttoned his vest under the sheepskin coat. That was the best he could do. It would just have to be enough.

He noticed that Walt Tomlin was observing him when he put the Ingersoll in his vest pocket and tucked the derringer into the opposite pocket with the fancy chain linking the two.

So his prisoner knew all there was to know about Longarm's weapons. That was a thing to keep in mind, no matter how agreeable and friendly the prisoner seemed to be at the moment.

"I'm ready," Longarm said.

Tomlin led the way out of the hotel room.

It took Longarm a moment to realize that, at least for the time being, control of the situation seemed to have passed to Walter Tomlin.

Chapter 6

Longarm could hardly believe the differences in Redcloud between the time when he had returned to the hotel and now, when he was trying to fight his way down the street to the railroad depot.

Before, it had been cold but certainly not unpleasant. Now the single street of Redcloud was a white, howling wilderness.

There were practically no lamps burning at this hour that Longarm could see. But then, he might well not have been able to see light across the street if one of the damned buildings had been on fire. The wind-driven snow was absolutely that thick.

Longarm had seen mountain snows before. He was no stranger to the storms that could sweep through. But if this one did not take the cake, then it was mighty close to it.

Huge, sloppy wet flakes were streaming in from the northwest, driven almost parallel to the ground even behind the protection of the surrounding mountains. What the wind and snow conditions would have been on an exposed northwest slope where some of the neighboring mines would be located was beyond Longarm's ability to comprehend.

Within seconds after stepping out of the hotel lobby onto the open street, his neck and cheeks stung. The right side of his face was quickly plastered with a growing accumulation of snow, and he could barely see out of his slitted right eye. His left eye smarted in the bite of the cold, and he had difficulty breathing, the roaring wind doing its best to suck the air from his lungs even as he tried to haul it in.

The bare earth and gravel of Redcloud's street was buried under immense and still growing drifts that lay downwind from every building, shed, water barrel, or any other form of obstruction. What little Longarm could see of the street scene looked like a series of stark white ocean waves.

Right shoulders lifted and hunched in futile protection for stinging, snow-packed ears, Longarm and Walter Tomlin crabbed their way forward through the storm. Longarm had to depend on Tomlin's sense of direction. He could see little more than white in any direction he looked, and if he had had to depend on finding the depot himself he could damn well have gotten lost and wound up floundering and defenseless in deep drifts. Men had been known to become confused and die of exposure within yards of shelter in conditions like these, Longarm knew. He could understand that more easily now. He was himself experiencing just such a sense of disorientation within fifty feet of leaving the hotel porch.

Tomlin, thank goodness, seemed to know where he was going. Even so, they had to wade knee-deep, hip-deep in some places, through one drift after another.

The night before, it would have been no more than an easy three-minute walk from the hotel to the depot. Now, after surely more than ten minutes of fighting the wind and the snow, Tomlin turned and shouted something to Longarm.

Longarm had no idea what the man was trying to say. Tomlin's words were whipped off his lips and carried downwind as fast as he could shout them. Longarm shook his head to signify that he could not hear.

Tomlin took Longarm's sleeve and tugged him to the right, away from the direction Longarm was sure the depot had to be.

Longarm had a momentary thought that his prisoner might be up to something. He flexed the cold fingers of his right hand inside the scant protection of his thin glove. But he followed where Tomlin led. There was damned little choice about that.

Tomlin pulled him to the right, over and through the deepest drift they had yet encountered.

As suddenly as if someone had thrown a lever the howl of the wind died, and they were out of the snow on bare earth again.

The wall of a dark building loomed above them, blocking the wind and spilling the snowdrift a few feet beyond it so that there was a tall white alley between the downwind wall of the structure and the terrible rising drifts. Off to their left Longarm could see the moving, swirling snow continue to accumulate. Tomlin used the heel of his hand to scrape some of the snow-plaster from the side of his face, and Longarm did the same. He was aware as he did so that already, after so few minutes, he had virtually no sensation of feeling in his right ear or along the jawline on that side of his face. He gulped cold air into his lungs, grateful that now the breath was not being pulled away from him.

"It's a bitch," Tomlin shouted. The words were unnecessarily loud now that there was no wind trying to carry the sounds away, and Tomlin blinked and looked slightly embarrassed. In a lower tone he added, "Worst I've ever seen, I think, and I sure thought I'd seen some."

"Do you know where we are?" Longarm asked.

"Hell, yes, don't you?"

Longarm shook his head.

"This is the mercantile," Tomlin said. He hooked a thumb over his shoulder to the glass window fronts, steamed and opaque now from the difference of temperatures indoors and out.

"But . . ." Longarm remembered seeing the store the previous day, but had not recognized it because there was a wooden sidewalk across the front of the place several feet higher than the street below. Stairs had been built to allow shoppers to gain access to the store. In reaching the sidewalk now they had not come up any steps. They had walked down off a snowdrift to get there. He shivered and used his left hand to clear some of the packed snow from inside the collar of his coat. The stuff was beginning to melt and drop icy rivulets of cold water under his shirt.

"What I think we'd best do," Tomlin said, "is stick beside the buildings on this side of the street. Between them and the drifts. We can scoot across the alleys easy enough, I think. We won't go back out into that shit until we're right across from the depot. Then I want you to hang onto my coattail, and we'll cross. Okay?"

Longarm nodded.

It was easier going that way, although the short periods of exposure to the wind between buildings seemed all the colder and all the worse after the relative warmth and calm of the protected lees of the town buildings.

Tomlin stopped in front of a saloon, empty of customers

63

at the moment, and shuttered against the storm with the light from a single lamp seeping out around the edges of the shutters and locked door, and hunched deeper into his coat. "Ready?" he asked.

"I reckon."

"Grab hold of my coat, then, and we'll go."

Longarm did as Tomlin suggested, and the railroad boss headed back out into the whip of the wind. Longarm held onto Tomlin's coat with his left hand and raised his right forearm to cover his exposed ear in a search for some measure of relief.

They bucked one drift and plunged up onto another, even larger one. Longarm's boot sank deep into the snow and he lost his balance. He fell, losing his grip on Tomlin's coat.

The prisoner could have chanced a break then, and there would have been little Deputy Long could have done to stop him short of shooting him in the back. And he would have had only seconds to accomplish that before Tomlin could have lost himself in the whiteout.

But Tomlin stopped, turned, and came back to grab Longarm by the shoulders and help pull him free of the dense drift. Tomlin leaned down to shout into Longarm's ear, "Lean on me, man. We're almost there."

Together the two men staggered forward, quartering away from the wind now, floundering hip-deep in clinging snow, until with a final effort Tomlin pulled Longarm into the lee of the depot wall. Apparently they had been on the covered platform for some moments, but Longarm had not been able to tell. The snow was driven under the roof just as hard as it had been driven across the open street, and Longarm had been aware of no difference at all. Once again they had to descend the drifts to reach the portion of the platform that had been protected from the drifting.

Longarm, shivering inside his thin coat, was glad for Tomlin's help as they lurched on numb feet to the door and tumbled inside, into the warmth that was being given off by the potbelly stove there.

The men straggled into the depot, crowding the small structure to capacity and smelling of wet wool and whiskey. There were more of them than Longarm would have thought for such a small spur line.

"It takes a lot," Jewett explained quietly to Longarm. "Not just warm bodies neither. You got to know what you're doing up here or you don't last long on Walt's section." He spoke with a certain amount of pride.

There was the day train crew, of course. The night crew members were the ones somewhere below, possibly trapped in the swirling whiteout that still raged outside the warm shack. The day men included the conductor, engineer, fireman, and two brakemen.

There was the clerk-stationmaster, who had guided Longarm to Tomlin's house the evening before, and the day and night telegraph operators. And there was the ground crew, a chief mechanic and his two assistants. And of course there was Walter Tomlin. About a dozen men in all.

"Are we all here?" Tomlin asked.

The door opened, admitting a gust of icy wind and a thin, greasy little man who was bundled into half a hundredweight of warm rags, and someone said, "Now we are."

Tomlin nodded.

The men had been busy talking among themselves, not loud but constant about it. Longarm noticed that Tomlin, despite his easygoing and friendly ways, did not have to raise his voice or announce himself to make the crew pay attention. When he spoke, they heard and were silent. The man was a hell of a good section chief, Longarm conceded, even if he was a thief.

"How does it look out there?" Tomlin asked the last man in.

"Like shit," the fellow answered. "It ain't slacked off a nickel's worth since it started. If anything, I'd say it's worse now than it was before."

Tomlin walked to the window and rubbed a bare spot in the condensation that was accumulating there. He stared out into the storm, although there was nothing to see outside but solid white. Dawn had already come, in theory. The only difference that seemed to make was to make the white swirls slightly paler.

"Walt?"

"Yes, Franklin?"

"I went by Miss Emma's like you asked. She said she'd have your sandwiches ready and send them over quick as she could, but there's not enough dried fruit to go around. And not much coffee neither. She said she'll substitute tea where she has to."

"All right." Tomlin sighed. "Until this slacks off," he mused aloud, "I can't take a rescue crew down. I just can't do it, boys. Too much chance of losing the tracks and getting lost in this shit."

"What is the situation?" Longarm asked.

Tomlin looked at him and blinked, as if he had forgotten who Longarm was and why he was present. Absently the man rubbed at his wrist where the handcuffs had chafed him during the night. He answered civilly enough, though.

"We have two engines assigned here," Tomlin said. "Both of them are somewhere down below. Could be they never left Silverton. Could be they're stuck somewhere. We can't know that with the telegraph down. If they're stranded it's up to us to rescue them. But we don't have any proper equipment for it. We have a plow, of course. A big-assed son of a bitch of a blade that we can mount on the front of one of the engines. But we don't have an engine to push the blade. What we got to work with up here now is shovels and a couple of handcarts." He sighed again. "No way we're gonna buck these drifts with a damned handcart. They're light little things anyhow, not enough weight to bull through a drift even if we could get that kind of speed from hand pumping, which we can't. So the way I see it, we got to wait here until we get a break in the weather and then try and make it down to the train on snowshoes. Then we'll have to break the train out and take it back to Silverton, or up here if it's close enough, and mount a plow. Prob'ly have to shift the engines so we have one facing out at each end of the train and a plow mounted at either end, like." He nodded to himself. Obviously, in addition to answering the question, he had been doing some thinking out loud, organizing the effort to his own satisfaction while he talked. "Yeah, I think that's what we'll need to do."

"How can you do that?" Longarm asked. "I didn't see a roundhouse at either end of the line."

"No roundhouse," Tomlin admitted, "but we built a half-assed sort of turntable up at this end, down at the end of the siding. We can get it done once we have the engines up this far."

"It'll be a bitch to dig out," one of the men said. "Do you want us to get started?"

Tomlin shook his head. "No point in that until the wind drops off. Dig out a drift now and the wind'd just build another. No, I think we have to wait until this storm dies. Then we can get something done. Meantime, Kent, I want you to go pick up those box lunches. Troy, Tony, Bob, you fellows go round up some snowshoes. Half a dozen of them anyway. Franklin, try that wire again, just to make sure."

The men began shifting, moving, pulling on coats and gloves. "No need for all of us to sit around here either," Tomlin continued. "The rest of you can go over to my house and fix yourselves some breakfast. Eat heavy, because it may be the last hot food any of us gets for a while." He gave them a tight smile and glanced once toward Longarm. "Help yourselves to anything you find there, boys. I won't be needing none of that food for a spell."

The men drifted out of the depot slowly, most of them giving Longarm dirty looks as they left. They too had seemed to have forgotten about what his presence here meant. The reminder from Walt Tomlin did not sit well with them.

Within a matter of minutes, Longarm was alone in the depot building with Tomlin and Franklin Jewett. Jewett tried the key again and shook his head. The line remained dead.

"Not much we can do now but wait for the wind to slack," Tomlin said. He removed his coat and draped it over the back of a chair, then helped himself to a seat. Jewett turned up the wick of the lamp beside his key and pulled a magazine from a desk drawer. The telegrapher seemed content enough to wait.

With a shiver that was more frustration than cold, Longarm settled in to wait for the howling of the wind to abate.

He smiled a little to himself. Back in Denver there would be no word of what was going on here, and if Longarm did not check in by evening Billy Vail was likely to shit green apples.

Still, there was no help for it. And, really, the assignment was still dead easy. He had his man in custody — more or less — and would present him to the court as soon as he could.

He yawned, not particularly worried about any of it. These mountain storms were fierce, he knew, but they always blew themselves out in a matter of hours. This one certainly could not last much longer.

He wondered how old the coffee was in that pot he could see keeping warm on top of the potbelly stove in the depot office.

Chapter 7

The man named Kent returned with two others, each of them laden with lunch packets wrapped in oilcloth, each of them half frozen and covered with snow. They stumbled their way into the room and huddled gratefully around the stove, their sodden clothes steaming.

"She didn't know how many to fix," Kent said, "so she made up two dozen lunches. Is that all right, Walt?"

Tomlin nodded. "The line can afford it." He smiled. "I hope." He motioned Longarm toward the packages that had been placed on top of the stationmaster's desk. "We might as well have something to eat. There seems to be plenty."

"That doesn't sound bad." He took one of the packages and handed another to Tomlin.

"Sit down, Longarm. Franklin, bring the marshal a cup of coffee, would you?"

Jewett laid his magazine aside and took down a tin cup

70

from a rack of them hanging on the back wall. He poured from the pot and brought the cup to Longarm.

"Thanks, I . . ."

Longarm felt a gust of cold wind on the back of his neck. The sound of the wind's roar swelled to fill the small room. A moment later both the sound and the blast of icy wind receded.

Longarm turned and felt a rush of hot anger drive through him.

Walter Tomlin was gone.

The man's coat remained on the chair where he had put it, but Tomlin was gone.

He had slipped outside while Longarm's attention was on the prospect of food and coffee.

Stupid, stupid son of a bitch, Longarm railed. He did not mean Walter Tomlin, he meant himself.

Tomlin had lulled him into inattention, and the son of a bitch had flown.

Longarm did not bother to dwell on thoughts about verbal paroles. Only fools believed in those anyway. But to be taken in so damned easily. . .

Longarm sat with the partially unwrapped packet of sandwiches in his hand and a foolish look on his face. He felt far more foolish than he ever could have looked.

One of the railroad crewmen, he realized, was in his shirtsleeves now. When Longarm sat down—where Tomlin had suggested, damn it—that man had still been wearing his coat. Tomlin's own gear was in plain sight, directly in front of Longarm. Behind Longarm's back, Tomlin had simply borrowed another coat and gone on his merry way.

Longarm set the package of food carefully down on the desk. There was no point in bolting to the closed door or in trying to catch Tomlin.

Not now. Through the nearly opaque windows he could

71

see the solid white wall of blowing snow. Visibility was virtually nonexistent out there. No one could hope to see more than a few yards in any direction, if that.

Tracks? With a wind like that, a man's tracks would be blown over and obliterated almost before his boot could be lifted out of the snow.

Tomlin knew the town and the country around it. He could have run in any direction, toward any hideyhole he knew of. That hideout could be only ten yards away and Longarm would never be able to follow him to it in conditions like these.

Son of a bitch, Longarm groaned inwardly. The man even had a package of sandwiches and coffee or tea with him.

He looked at the other men in the room, but their expressions were blank. Deliberately so? He could not tell. They might have been in on this as an escape plan all along. He would probably never know.

He kept his own expression as blank as theirs, not willing to give them the satisfaction of seeing him so angry about this. Inside . . . that was another story. Inside he was seething, both at himself and at Walt Tomlin.

Call me Walt, Longarm. You got my word on it, Longarm. I done it and you caught me fair and square, Longarm.

Shit!

Deliberately hiding his feelings from the railroad men in the office, Longarm retrieved the package of food, opened it, and pulled out a sandwich. He took a bite and chewed slowly. It wasn't bad. Ham with some sort of prepared sauce that had a sharp bite to it. He took a sip of the coffee Jewett had brought him. How much of this had Jewett been in on? he wondered. The coffee was stale and bitter on his tongue. On the other hand, perhaps it was something else that was so damned bitter. He smiled and nodded at Jewett, raising the cup silently in his direction.

"Thanks, Franklin."

Jewett smiled back at him. Pretty damned smugly, Longarm thought.

"You're welcome, Marshal. Any time." The smile spread out and became a grin.

Longarm pushed back an impulse to throw the hot, bitter coffee in Jewett's smug face. Outwardly he only nodded pleasantly and took another sip.

Longarm put his coat and gloves on and left the depot quietly. Almost as quietly as Walter Tomlin had, damn him. Longarm sighed. *Damn him*. In spite of all of Longarm's experience, the slippery bastard had gulled him into thinking he was a no-problem prisoner. When would he ever learn that there was no such animal? Men became prisoners of the law because they were criminals; criminals were not to be trusted. Longarm wondered if he would remember that better if he beat himself over the head and recited it out loud fifty times.

Now he was going to have to find the son of a bitch and drag him back to Denver, kicking and screaming if necessary. Come to think of it, kicking and screaming might be preferable. At least then Longarm would have an excuse to work out some of his frustrations on the man.

Longarm shook his head, angry with himself all over again. No, that attitude would not do any good either. There were some things a man just did not do, not if he had any pride. It would be too much like spurring a horse just because the rider had screwed up and was angry with himself.

The hell with it, Longarm thought. Tomlin was still somewhere in Redcloud. That was for sure. No one was going anywhere in this weather.

He would just have to put the cuffs on the bastard again. And this time keep them there.

Longarm took a deep breath and turned the collar of his coat higher. He was standing in the lee of the depot, wind roaring past with almost unbelievable ferocity. He knew the station platform was roofed, but the wind-borne snow was too dense for him to see it and it certainly offered no shelter from the storm. Come to think of it, he decided, he knew the platform *had* been roofed. For all he could see now, the damn thing might have blown away during the night.

Standing there, even out of the wind with the building at his back, he was becoming quickly chilled. The only thing he was accomplishing here was to get out of the sight of those smirking railroad employees, the ones who had stood there and laughingly watched him lose his prisoner. He had to move along, and soon, or the intense cold of the false shelter would begin to sap his strength. He had made quite enough mistakes for one day, and he did not particularly want to die in the main street of Redcloud, Colorado, lost in a blizzard only feet away from heat and comfort.

He felt his way along the front of the building and around the side, into the full force of the icy wind, until he reached the back corner of the depot. That, he remembered, was on the street side. Immediately in front of him, although he could not see it, was the line of storefronts that faced the railroad tracks. They could not be more than thirty or forty yards off.

Looking out into the teeth of the storm was like trying to see a penny dropped into the bottom of a pot of green pea

74

soup. He knew the stores had to be out there. He just could not see where.

He paused there for a moment to get his bearings, trying to ignore the crust of wet, heavy snow that was building on the left side of his face, nearly closing his left eye already.

The wind was quartering down on him from the left and front. If he kept going into it exactly that way—and if there were no gusting shifts of direction while he was out on the street—he should be able to walk straight across to the saloon where he and Tomlin had stopped before.

Damn the man, Longarm thought again. He could have gotten away earlier, when they were crossing toward the depot, when Longarm went down and could have been in serious trouble if Tomlin had not helped him. Instead the bastard had made sure that Longarm was all right, then he made his break.

Warmed for the moment by his anger, Longarm left the security of the railroad station and plunged forward into the freezing wind and blowing snow.

He could have covered the distance in seconds at a run, but the ever-deepening drifts would not allow him to run. The snow was so deep and yet so yielding, like wading hip-deep in a muddy-bottomed lake, that he was barely able to keep his balance at a walk.

Step by leg-weary step he slogged forward, maintaining the wind on his left cheek. Breathing was difficult. Snow driving against his face kept clogging his nostrils so that he had to breathe through his mouth. The taste of the melting snow was sharp on his tongue. Within half a minute or less he could no longer feel the wind on his numbed cheek, and his left eye burned, feeling curiously hot under the onslaught of the cold wind.

If he lost feeling there, if he no longer was able to judge

the angle of the wind striking him and shifted direction . . .

Longarm shook his head and plunged stubbornly forward through the storm, gasping and staggering, tiring after only minutes of exposure. He could not really imagine what it would be like to be caught far from shelter in a storm like this one. He did not *want* to know.

Time passed with agonizing slowness, measured not in seconds or minutes but by footsteps, each lift and reach of his booted feet an uphill battle against the elements.

Eventually the wind lessened in its drive against him. It probably was no more than two minutes at the outside, although it felt like half of forever.

His face was so numbed that he could not really be sure of the reduction of force by that gauge. Instead he felt a lessening of the wind pressure against his chest. He was able to stand more nearly upright, no longer having to lean forward to maintain his balance against the shove and push of the hard wind.

He rubbed a gloved hand over his face to scrape away some of the snow and stumbled blindly into the wall of the saloon.

"Found it, by damn," he muttered, half in satisfaction at achieving the crossing and half in annoyance at having made the discovery by walking into the side of a blank wall. He supposed it was amusing enough, really, but when he tried to smile about it he felt the pull of cold, cracking lips and the rigidity of ice that was frozen tight to his moustache.

He felt his way along the wall to a window and saw that while the shutters over the windows were still firmly in place there was more light inside now than there had been earlier, and there seemed to be activity in there too. Longarm made his way to the door, pushed it open, and went inside to find light, warmth, and people. The heat felt stifling, but damned welcome, after the intense cold outside.

Men at the bar turned to look at him curiously, probably unsure of who he might be under that thick crust of wet, packed snow.

Longarm smiled at them. "Hell of a beautiful spring morning, huh?"

Someone chuckled and raised a steaming mug in his direction.

"Hot rum toddy, friend?" the bartender asked. "They seem to be right popular today."

Longarm nodded and began to strip some of the snow from his face and arms. Right now a hot rum toddy sounded better to him than a wagonload of the best Maryland rye would have. Right now a hot rum toddy sounded like just about the very best thing ever devised by humankind.

"I think," Longarm said, "you just saved my life."

"Sure an' you can pay me what it's worth then, friend," the barman said. He picked up a steaming kettle and poured boiling water into a tin cup already prepared with dark rum and a spoonful of brown sugar.

Longarm took a deep draught of the toddy, his lips so numb from the cold that he did not at all mind the contact with the steaming beverage. The heat of it reached his stomach and spread through him. "Just what the doctor ordered."

Chapter 8

Longarm felt better, much better, after several of those welcome hot toddies and a huge breakfast in the hotel restaurant. At least the hotel, being on the same side of the street as the saloon, was not so very difficult to reach. It seemed that until the storm abated, though, the only places he could comfortably get to would be those on this same side of the single business street of Redcloud.

As for Walter Tomlin, he could damned well wait until the storm subsided. Neither of them was going very far until then.

Longarm ate, then went up to his room to change into dry socks and the moccasins he carried in his bag. Leather boots, no matter how comfortable or well made, were not a match for this kind of weather.

Sitting around the hotel lobby did nothing to make him feel any better about this situation. He was itchy to get

Tomlin back into custody and get on with it. Ten minutes of trying to read an elderly copy of the *Rocky Mountain News* was about all he could stand of that. He crossed the lobby to the desk, fortunately manned now by a different clerk than the disapproving gent of the evening before, and asked, "Do you have any idea where I could find Walt Tomlin?" So much for the idea of letting it slide until the storm ended.

"This time of day and the weather being like it is, sir, I'd say you should try at the depot. If you think you can make it over there. Me, I'd wait if I was you."

"As a matter of fact I've already asked there."

The clerk thought that over for a moment. "They tell me that Mr. Tomlin is pretty conscientious about his work." *Mister* Tomlin, Longarm noted. It was interesting to discover that not quite everyone in Redcloud could be expected to side with the thieving railroad boss. "I expect there wouldn't be anything he could do right now, though. Tell you where I'd look for him if I was you, mister." The man grinned, "Same place I'd be if I wasn't on duty this morning. Weather like this there's nothing better'n to snuggle up next to something warm and willing, if you know what I mean." He gave Longarm a wink.

Longarm grinned back at him. "That isn't a bad idea, friend. Any suggestions?"

The clerk shrugged. "There's a hell of a lot to choose from around here. A man like Mr. Tomlin now, he wouldn't be going to one of them crib girls. Not that they're so likely to be easy found in a storm anyhow, the cribs being as poor built as they are." Longarm got the impression that the clerk must have had some experience with the fifty-cent girls himself, to be so well acquainted with their quarters. "So what I'd suggest would be for you to check along the row. The bigger houses, you see."

Longarm glanced over his shoulder toward the wind that was still raging just beyond the hotel windows. "Which side of the street would that be on?"

"This side, mister. You wouldn't have to cross over."

"Thanks."

The clerk peered over the counter toward Longarm's moccasined feet. "If you want, mister, I could give you the loan of some proper footgear for this kind of weather. Folks leave the damnedest things in hotel rooms, you know, and we got a pile of stuff in the basement. I likely could dig you up something better'n those skins."

"Why, I'd appreciate that."

The clerk shrugged. "No trouble." He disappeared and returned several minutes later with an armful of boots for Longarm to choose from. An ugly but warm-looking pair of buffalo-hide overboots with the curly, dark wool left on the inside of the crude pouches did the trick nicely, fitting over Longarm's moccasins with ease.

Longarm thanked the man and left, feeling much better prepared for the weather. Outside, he thought the visibility was perhaps a little better than it had been earlier. The sun was well up, somewhere above the solid, stormy overcast, and there was light enough. And at least in the lee of the commercial buildings there was little enough snow in the air that he could see from one end of the block to the other, although anything taking place across the street was still as good as invisible. The only times he was really uncomfortable was when he crossed the alley mouths between the buildings and building blocks.

Few of the stores he passed had bothered to open for business, but by now all of the saloons—and they seemed to make up fully half of the businesses in Redcloud—were doing a booming trade. Longarm guessed that none of the mine shifts would be working today, so the off-duty population of the town was probably twice what it would normally be.

Though he could see many people inside the buildings, there were practically none out on the sidewalk. Twice he passed heavily bundled men making their way to favored saloons, and both of those fellows looked as miserable as Longarm himself had felt just a little while before.

He hunched deeper into his coat.

The saloons gave way within four blocks to a row of multi-story houses set close together in a separate block of their own. He might have mistaken them for residences except for the red-frosted glass in the lanterns that were mounted on either side of their fancy doorways. The lanterns were not lighted at this time of day, but the color of the glass was apparent just the same. Longarm leaned into the force of the wind and made his way to the nearest of the whorehouses.

"Go away," was the response he got to his pounding on the first door. "We ain't open this early." Longarm continued to hammer on the door until it was yanked open by a frizzy-haired old bawd who must surely have been the madam. He could not imagine such an ugly creature making a living at whoring, not even in a mining camp.

"I want . . ." he began.

"Get the fuck outa here, I tole you," the old hag screeched. "We ain't open." She tried to slam the door on him, but Longarm stuck his foot through, remembered in time that he did not want to catch the sharp edge of the door on a foot protected only by a moccasin and soft overboot, and caught the door with his knee instead.

Any good humor he might have had had already vanished in the storm with Walter Tomlin. He forced his way inside, ignoring the screamed protests of the old bitch, and pulled his wallet out.

"This is an official visit," he snapped. "We can handle it nice and peaceable while we sit in your parlor, or I can cart you down to the jail and do it that way."

The old bawd underwent a quick adjustment of attitude. She blinked rapidly for a moment, then gave him what was probably her best attempt at a grandmotherly simper and a nearly toothless smile. "Why, sure, honey. I haven't done nothing wrong, have I?"

"It's called obstructing justice," Longarm said wearily, "and I can sure make it stick if I have to."

She gave him a smile of sweet reason. "No need for that, honey. Come right in and set in the parlor." Her voice was honey-coated.

She took him in, took his coat and hat, and led him to a soiled sofa in the front room. It was the kind of place where a man necessarily entertained thoughts of rare diseases when he saw it in daylight. He sat gingerly on the edge of the cleanest-looking cushion.

From farther back in the scuzzy house he could hear occasional movement, but there was no sign of the "ladies" who inhabited the place. That was probably just as well, he thought, if their madam was any example of the goods available here.

"One second, honey," the old whore said softly. She turned and shouted in a rasping voice, "Earl. Earl! Get your black ass out here. Where the fuck are you, Earl?"

"Ma'am?" Earl turned out to be a scrawny Negro of advanced age and gentle expression. If the old fellow's duties included that of being the house bouncer, Longarm hoped he had one hell of a big shotgun, because he did not look big enough or vigorous enough to overpower an enraged mouse.

"Bring the gennelmun some coffee," the woman said grandly. To Longarm she added. "A little sweetener in your coffee, Deputy? Bourbon? Rye?"

"No, thanks." The old bat might look a mess, but she had not missed the specifics of his office when she glanced at that badge, he noticed. She remembered exactly who and what he was.

"Or something else to get you warm, honey?" She batted her eyes and smiled. "I have the most lovely young ladies to satisfy any taste. French. Greek. Or something exotic? I have just the *sweetest* little Injun girl that likes it rough. Anything you want, Deputy, and no charge to a fine gennelmun like you, of course."

"No, thank you," Longarm said.

"You will take coffee, won't you?"

"Uh, no." The mere fact of boiling the stuff would not be enough to make him feel comfortable consuming anything in this place. The thought of it was enough to make a man shudder.

"Then what can I do for you, dearie?"

Earl faded silently away toward the back of the house.

"I'm looking for Walter Tomlin."

The old broad rearranged her wrinkles into a sour expression. "Huh! Tomlin don't ever come here. As if my ladies wasn't fancy enough for him. You won't find him here, let me tell you."

"You wouldn't mind if I looked for myself, would you?"

"Hell, look all you want. I don't give a shit. But you won't find him. Not here. If you want that hoity-toity bastard, look over to Emma's place. That's where he trades."

83

"Miss Emma's?"

"Yeah, that's the place." She made a sour face again and looked like she wanted to spit. Apparently Miss Emma was not a close friend of hers.

Longarm had heard the name before, in connection with the lunches ordered for the railroad crew, but he had naturally assumed that Miss Emma ran a restaurant. Apparently the food was an extra service the lady could offer.

He thought about it, didn't want to do it, considered any number of excuses to avoid it, but eventually concluded that since he was here already he really would have to go through with a search of the premises for the missing Mr. Tomlin. There were things he really would rather have done.

But excuses didn't catch felons, and if Tomlin was hiding out in this place Longarm did not want to give the man another opportunity to slip away.

And just because this bad-smelling hag said Tomlin was not there, it did not necessarily follow that he really was not there. Longarm was just going to have to close his nose to the smells of the place and do his duty.

He stood and fingered the Colt at his waist. There was no point in putting it off. Better to get this done with as quickly as possible.

"E-excuse me. Please," Longarm stammered. He took half a step backward and swept his hat off, despite the cold and the snow that was spilling down over him in an eddying current of wind moving across the roof of the house. "I must have . . . made a mistake."

He was embarrassed and probably blushing as well. How could he have known that there would be a respectable home set in the midst of Redcloud's whorehouse row? He could not have guessed, of course, but he felt embarrassed just the same to have intruded on the privacy and the dignity of such a lovely woman as this delicate female.

Delicate she was, and lovely, too. She was blonde, slender, and patrician, with skin like ivory and features that looked as if they had been taken from a masterpiece of sculpture and breathed into life. She wore a tasteful gown of a blue-gray satin that exactly matched the color of her eyes and had on a brooch and matching pair of earrings that were possibly the loveliest cameos Longarm had ever seen. Yet the cameos could not begin to match the beauty of their owner.

"Excuse me," he said again.

The blonde vision smiled at him with serene composure, slightly exposing perfectly formed teeth between full and perfectly bowed red lips.

"I am Miss Emma," the vision said in a voice as lovely as her appearance. "Whom did you wish to see, sir?"

Longarm blinked, stunned. There wasn't a hell of a lot that could shake him. At least he had not thought there could be. But this did.

This was Miss Emma? The madam? Incredible. She looked like a senator's lady.

On the other hand, Custis Long had had occasion to meet a fair number of senators' ladies in the course of his duties. This stunning woman looked the way a senator's lady *ought* to look. She looked like the ante-bellum belle of the finest mansion of the South.

She looked . . . hell, she looked damn good.

Longarm clamped his jaw shut—it seemed to have been sagging for a moment there—and took that half-step back again. *"You* are Miss Emma?"

Emma laughed, a delightful sound reminiscent of chimes and summer days, and her eyes sparkled. "I believe, sir, that I have received a compliment. Thank you, whoever you are. Would you come inside? This weather is too brisk for chatting at the door."

Half numb again, but this time not from the cold, Longarm accepted the invitation.

The inside of the house, unlike the other three he had so far visited along the row, was in its own way as lovely as Miss Emma was. Elegant, grand, expensive, and tasteful.

A butler, balding and severe in morning coat and spats, appeared behind the mistress of the house to accept Longarm's hat and coat, then disappeared as silently as he had come. This house was not for the muckers and moles who worked underground in the dirty, dangerous mine shafts. Miss Emma definitely catered to the carriage trade, such as it might be in Redcloud.

Miss Emma led him into her parlor and seated him in a sinfully comfortable chair, then herself poured and served him a snifter of fine and ancient brandy. Longarm accepted the drink without thought, automatically, even though he had no taste at all for brandies.

The lady of the establishment—he thought of her as such, even knowing what she did for her livelihood—sat nearby, lowering herself into the chair with all the grace of royalty assuming a throne.

"Let me see," Miss Emma said in a throaty, sensual voice. "You would be Deputy Marshal Long." She smiled. "May I call you Longarm?"

"Please." He still was not over the shock.

She continued to smile at him and sat patiently, with no sign of worry or nervousness, with her back straight, chin high, and hands calmly folded in her lap.

Miss Emma's figure, he noted, was as perfect as her face, its curves exactly right, neither too much nor too little. Looking at her would be enough to make a parson pant and paw the ground.

"How may I help you, Longarm?" she asked.

Longarm swallowed, blinked, and took a small sip of the brandy. For brandy, it really wasn't bad.

Damn it, though, he wasn't some wide-eyed schoolkid getting a look at a grownup woman for the very first time. And Miss Emma, no matter how beautiful she was, was still and all a whorehouse madam. He told himself to shape up and remember that.

"First," he said, "how does it happen that you know who I am?" He made his voice deliberately harsh and grating.

Miss Emma was unshaken, her poise undisturbed. "In my business, Longarm, I make it a point to be fully informed of the goings-on in town. In particular about those matters which concern my best customers. It is no secret, I believe, that dear Walter has been a very good customer here. I daresay I knew about you within five minutes of Walter's arrest last night."

"Have you seen Walter this morning?" Longarm asked. "Or heard from him?"

"Yes," Miss Emma said without hesitation. She continued to smile at him.

"Which?"

"I beg your pardon?"

"Which one? Have you seen him, or just heard from him?"

"I see. I have heard from him."

"But you haven't seen him?"

"No, I have not."

"Why should I believe that?" Feeling more in control now, he sat back in the comfortable chair and swirled the brandy in the bottom of the snifter. He took another sip, then set the glass aside and reached for a cheroot without asking Emma's permission. Not, by damn, in a whorehouse, regardless of the woman's bearing and beauty.

Emma chuckled. If she did not find the question amusing, she was giving a damned good imitation of it. "My dear man, if I dissemble, and am caught at it, I am sure you would not hesitate to prosecute me for obstruction of justice."

Longarm's expression did not change, but he felt a sudden rise of interest. How could she have known anything about the threat he had made to that first madam? He was sure no one had passed him on the street when he was making the tour from one house to the next. At least, he was almost sure. He had seen no one, had seen no tracks in the relatively wind-free areas downwind of the house fronts. Yet there had been times when he had been away from the front windows of several places while he was searching inside them for Tomlin.

A woman of such obvious quality and intelligence just might have come to know something about the law during her years of close association with the wealthy and the powerful. Her use of the phrase did not necessarily mean that she had already received information from down the street. But it could mean that she had.

Longarm did not take time to ponder the many possibilities suggested by her wording. He covered a moment of thought by lighting his cheroot, then asked, "Do you know where Walt is right now?"

"No," Miss Emma said easily. She looked over Longarm's shoulder and snapped her fingers. A young girl, quite an attractive morsel herself, brought a hand-painted ceramic ashtray and set it at Longarm's elbow, then quietly withdrew from the room. The girl wore a maid's black dress with white apron and white cap, but the dress was scandalously short and exposed dark stockings filled with very shapely legs. Longarm found himself wondering just what manner of services the maid could be called upon to provide.

"You don't know where he is, then?" he asked.

"I have said that I do not, sir."

"And I am expected to believe you."

"Yes." She nodded, still completely composed.

Longarm smiled at her. "Then of course I shall, Miss Emma."

Miss Emma nodded again, coolly, apparently finding it completely natural that her word should be accepted.

"Do you screw Walter yourself?" Longarm asked.

He had expected to jolt her, to find a crack in that cool composure. Instead, Miss Emma fielded the question with every bit as much aplomb as if he had asked the pattern of her silver service.

"From time to time," she answered. "My personal fees are quite high, and he could afford them only rarely."

"No free fun for good old Walt?"

She smiled at him. She still seemed to find this whole thing a mildly amusing episode. "Never," she said pleasantly. "Not for anyone."

Longarm was beginning to get the impression that he— that any man—was out of his depth with this ice maiden.

He was also beginning to realize that he was not going to learn a damned thing here beyond what the beauteous Miss Emma wanted him to know, however much or however little that might be. Curiosity, though, forced him to ask one more question. "What are your fees, Miss Emma?"

The woman laughed. "Is that a professional question, Longarm? Or a personal one?"

"Call if personal, though I'm just window shopping. Government employees don't make all that much."

"As you wish, Longarm. The fee for my personal services is fifty dollars hourly or three hundred for the night."

He whistled and rolled his eyes.

"I've never had a complaint," she added with a wink. "For future reference, Longarm, my young ladies are highly skilled, and are available at a more conveniently affordable level. And I would be glad to accept a government voucher in payment."

Longarm raised an eyebrow. "Correct me if I'm wrong, but I don't think the eyeshade and sleeve-garter boys would approve payment for girls."

"But they do for meal services, Longarm. Keep that in mind." She laughed softly.

A light dawned and he asked, "Do you provide much in the way of . . . uh . . . meal services for the railroad?"

"From time to time," she admitted readily.

Just another of Walter Tomlin's little thieving tricks, Longarm guessed. Not that that was of interest to the Justice Department. It was hardly a federal matter. Still, it was something he would pass along to the railroad for their auditors to take a look at. Good old Walt could find himself serving a federal stretch and then a state one on top of that if the railroad chose to prosecute.

Longarm stood. He had not been aware of being watched, yet within seconds the butler was in the doorway with Longarm's coat and hat in hand. He took a step in that direction, then turned back toward Miss Emma. "Would you do something for me?"

"Within limits. You may certainly ask."

"Could you get a message to Walter?"

"Yes." Again there was no hesitation whatsoever. He was not sure if this woman was for real or not. Regardless, she must be a master at covering her own ass. No matter how the pursuit of Walter Tomlin came out, there would damn sure be nothing incriminating about her that he could take to a judge.

"Tell him for me that it's not too late. He can still turn himself in without prejudice."

"I shall tell him," she said.

"Thanks." He took another step, paused, and turned back again. "Would you have any objection if I searched your premises?"

"None whatsoever. Henry will guide you." The woman seemed totally unflappable.

Longarm gave up. There was no way he was going to rattle this one. Meekly he took his coat and hat and then followed the butler on what he was absolutely positive would be a fruitless search of Miss Emma's house of high-quality whores.

And he was right about that, the classy attractiveness of the surroundings, animate and otherwise, notwithstanding.

Chapter 9

By the time Longarm came out of the last of the houses on the row, not surprisingly without having found Tomlin, the sky was no longer a solid mass of low, dark, scudding cloud and snow. Instead, above a ground-hugging level of blowing snow, the sky was very nearly the color of Miss Emma's eyes, pale and as much blue as gray. The worst of the storm seemed to be breaking, although the wind continued to blow, picking up and rearranging the snow that had fallen earlier. A thin, watery sunlight filtered down through the breaking clouds and the ground blizzard of moving snow. The impression of its warmth was probably false, but Longarm found himself standing taller and walking straighter now than he had been, no longer hunched and huddled against the bite of the storm.

Others were beginning to appear on the street too, darting quickly from storefront to storefront, but willing to move about now, where before they had holed up close to a stove and remained indoors.

For the first time since the storm began, Longarm could look down the street and see a full city block at a time, although anything beyond that distance remained obscured by the continued swirl of the ground blizzard.

He hurried past the row of whorehouses he had just visited, still holding close to the lee of the structures so he would be out of the wind, and crossed a wide alley mouth, almost a street itself, to the next block of buildings.

Out in the street the drifts had built so high that he could not see the sidewalks or storefronts of the buildings facing him on that far side of the street. He was able to see only second-floor windows and the tops of false building fronts over the drifts. Nowhere along the street, he judged, had the drifts accumulated to less than seven or eight feet. And in some places, in front of the open alleys where the wind had had no blockage until it came up short against the buildings on the far side of the street, the drifts were ten feet or more in depth.

All of that had happened in fifteen hours or possibly less. It was barely past noon now, and Redcloud was virtually buried. It was a hell of an example of a mountain storm, Longarm thought. Springtime in the Rockies.

Longarm walked past saloons and gaming halls, hardware stores and a haberdashery, the mercantile and more saloons.

The few men he passed were for the most part moving from one saloon to another. He saw no women on the street at all.

As he neared the saloon he knew to be opposite the railroad depot, a small man with a woolen cap pulled low over his forehead reeled out of the place, staggered, and grabbed at Longarm's arm for support.

"Easy now." Longarm automatically helped the drunk to regain his balance, then stood looking down into the smaller man's rheumy eyes. "G'day, Sheriff," Longarm muttered.

The sheriff tilted his head back to take a look at this tall stranger, swayed, and almost lost his balance again. Longarm steadied him with a grab at the man's arm.

Maxwell blinked. It seemed to take him a moment to focus his eyes. "Do I know you? Wait. Don't tell me now. I remember." He smiled, pleased with himself. "I do remember you. A deputy. From Silverton? Can't recall your name, though." He giggled. "You all look alike, you know." The sheriff clamped his lips shut, and his cheeks bulged briefly as he tried to contain a burp. He still had not shaved—probably a good thing, Longarm thought; the man would have been a menace with a razor—and he still smelled of whiskey, both old and fresh.

Longarm tried to keep the distaste he felt out of his expression. Gently he tried to steady the man and turn him in the direction down the sidewalk toward which he had been uncertainly heading.

"Don't be pushing at me, you young son of a bitch," Maxwell snapped.

"What?"

"Don't you be pushing at me, damn you. Think you can come in here an' do whatever you want. Bullshit. This here's my juriz...jurish...jurisdiction, damn you. You don't do shit here without me sayin' you can. You got that? Damn well better." The man's voice rose and fell from angry shout to slurred mumble. "I was wearin' a badge when you was still puking your mama's milk, boy. Don't you forget that. I'm no damned country hick. I'm Evan Maxwell, an' I'm the law here." He blinked rapidly several times and refocused on an amazed Longarm. "You got no power to arrest nobody here. Nobody."

Maxwell set his unshaven jaw in a pugnacious jut and glared up at Longarm. The effect was somewhat spoiled when the man swayed, lost his balance again, and nearly fell.

Longarm righted him once more and opened his mouth to speak, but he did not know what he could say to this drunken banty rooster. It damn sure was no time to bother arguing law and federal powers.

"I'll remember that, Sheriff," Longarm said gently.

"See you do, you son of a bitch." Maxwell blinked and shoved his jaw forward again.

That was not language that rode easy on a man's belly, but Longarm remained unruffled. He had no idea what had gotten into the poor old drunk's craw. Likely just the man's own devils chasing around and around inside a pickled skull. Longarm felt pity for him rather than anger.

Longarm considered trying to help Maxwell to wherever he was going, probably to the next saloon on the block, then realized that in the sheriff's current state that might be unwise. He turned and walked quietly away from the swaying, blinking souse.

He headed across the street, and was knee-deep in heavy snow within a few feet of the clear area along the building fronts, then as quickly hip-deep in the clinging stuff.

The snow was wet and dense enough that he had to climb the drifts instead of wading through them. It was hard work, and he was grateful for the loan of the buffalo-hide boots long before he was halfway across the drifted street.

From the saloon across the way the only thing he had been able to see of the single-story depot building was its stovepipe. From out on the drifts themselves he could see that the station platform had been drifted solid with snow along much of its length, and down at the far end, away from the depot office, it looked like the weight of that snow had buckled a portion of the roof. Longarm turned to his right. He was going to have to fight his way across more drifts and go around the end of the building to reach the door. The wind continued to blow, carrying already fallen snow with it, but the sky was definitely clearer overhead.

He floundered and fought his way down off the drift he had been climbing and started up the next one. The drifts lay angled across the street like so many waves frozen onto an ocean surface, long windrows with valleys between them.

The wind was not quite so bad now, he thought. At least he was no longer having so much trouble breathing against the force of it.

He started up the side of the next drift, feeling the pull of the exertion at high altitude deep in his heaving chest and lungs. This was damned difficult work.

As he neared the crest of the last drift he paused for a moment's breather and knelt in the wet, yielding snow.

Beside his left hand a small, perfectly round hole appeared in the surface of the snow.

Longarm looked at it, uncomprehending for a moment. He pulled the hand away and peered closer at the odd hole, which was quickly drifting shut.

Another hole appeared not far from the first. This time he was watching when it hit. The snow dimpled inward without any hint of sound over the force of the wind.

Longarm threw himself backward, somersaulting down the slope of the drift and out of sight.

Some son of a bitch was shooting at him.

Longarm had heard absolutely nothing. Not a muzzle report, not a whine of the bullets, certainly not an impact in the soft white snow of the drift.

The bullets had struck just downwind of him. Probably the man with the gun had aimed square in the middle of his back. Tomlin? One of Tomlin's friends?

The wind had been strong enough to carry the bullet's flight wide.

Longarm came to his hands and knees in the valley between the drifts, his Colt in his hand, searching for a target.

He scrambled up the side of the drift he had just come down, but by then he was much too late.

The shots could have come from nearly anywhere— from the street, a roof, any of the blankly staring second-story windows he could see back up the street.

He could see Sheriff Evan Maxwell weaving his way to the door of another saloon.

Down the block a man was coming out of the mercantile. The man paused at the door to speak to someone inside the place, then came out onto the exposed portion of the sidewalk. He nodded pleasantly to the sheriff, who continued on in his deliberate, stiff-legged gait.

There was no one else. No one that Longarm could see.

Yet somewhere out there, behind one of those windows or around some building corner, he felt that there were eyes on him. Watching. Waiting. And there was a gun in the watcher's hand.

Longarm felt cold. He shoved the big Colt back into his holster and tried to attribute the feeling to the wind that was trickling under the tail of his sheepskin coat and trying to creep its way past his upturned collar.

He was not entirely sure that he believed that himself, but he gave it a whirl.

Wary now, he turned and once again looked for a way through to the depot office.

The railroad office was empty except for the day telegraph operator, a man Longarm had seen that morning but whose name he either had not heard or could not now remember. There was no sign of Jewett, although the night telegrapher's magazine lay face down on a corner of the key desk. The day operator gave Longarm a blank, neutral look when Longarm came inside and stamped the snow from his boots.

"Where is everybody?" Longarm asked.

The telegrapher shrugged. "Mostly over at Tomlin's, I'd think. Or sleeping. Once the weather breaks and they got to start out it's gonna be a hell of a hard push, and no telling for how long. They'll need all the rest they can get, and they know it."

Longarm looked out through the window, trying to see up through the low layer of windblown snow toward the sky. The lower level of fast scud had broken. Above it, very high, there was a thin layer of scattered cloud with bright blue showing around and through it. "Looks to me like it's broken," Longarm observed. "Shouldn't they be coming in now?"

"They already been back once," the telegrapher said. "Half an hour, maybe forty-five minutes ago. Tomlin sent word they should hole up again an' sleep until the danger's past."

There it was again, Longarm thought. An open admission that Walt Tomlin was still in touch. Federal warrant or no, Tomlin continued to call the shots here.

"I'd have thought the danger *was* past," Longarm said.

The telegrapher grunted and crooked a finger, beckoning Longarm toward a small window set high in the side of the building. "C'mere."

Longarm gave the man a quick, questioning look, but the telegrapher seemed at ease, and he had no visible weapons. "All right."

Barely visible above a massive drift that ran along the southwest side of the station, the window looked up toward one of the jagged peaks that towered above Redcloud.

"You see the Goat Horns up there?" the telegrapher asked.

"If you mean those two dark spires on the near side of that peak, yes."

"You see how they're two dark tips with white under and between them, then."

Longarm nodded.

"That right there is the danger, mister."

"I don't understand," Longarm said.

The telegrapher grunted again. "Maybe you wouldn't at that, not being familiar with this country, but the thing is, long as I've been here I've never before seen snow deep enough or wet enough to stick on that side of the Goat Horns. They're three, maybe four times as tall as what you can see there. And that area between them, that's steep rock too. Always bare, even in the worst kind of winter. Except right now it's full of snow. Heavy, wet snow. There's a hell of a lot of weight laying up there, man."

"Yes?"

"Below the Horns . . . I don't guess you can see it from here 'cause of the drift outside the window, but just below the Horns there's an old avalanche chute. Not a twig on it though God only knows how long it's been since there was a slide from up at the Goat Horns. An' that chute, it runs right down to the road, mister. When that stuff comes down, an' you can bet your ever-livin' soul that it *will* come down, it'll wipe out anything that's in its path. *Everything,* be it man or machine, mister. Nobody in his right mind would try and move out of here until the Horns shed that slide."

Longarm took another look at the distant precipice. There was only blue sky above it now, not a hint of snow in the air around it, but a white plume that could have been mistaken for smoke was blowing off the slab of heavy snow that lay between the Goat Horns. The snow might have abated, but the wind was still busy up there.

"That's why Tomlin sent the word that he did, mister," the telegraph operator continued. "It wouldn't be any kind of safe to send a crew out with that hanging over them. It would be like putting them right underneath Damocles's sword and then having somebody swipe at the thread with a razor."

"I think it was a hair," Longarm mumbled, his attention on the Goat Horns. He was trying to decide it this information was fact, or a bluff that might be intended to make him think Tomlin would have to stay put in Redcloud while good old Walt made an escape.

"What?" the operator asked.

"I think it was a hair they used to hang that sword from, not a thread."

"Oh. Well, you see what I mean, anyhow."

"Yeah, I do." Longarm pulled his gloves back on and buttoned his coat. The heat of the place was welcome, but he did not seem to be accomplishing anything here.

"There won't be any of our boys moving until the Horns shed their snow, Marshal," the telegrapher said. "An' I don't figure to lie to you about that. Even if I might've otherwise, which I wouldn't, Tomlin sent word that none of us was to do anything that we could get arrested for.

That's why he isn't letting any of us know where he is, so we can't any of us be accused of harboring a fugitive."

Someone had to know, Longarm thought, or all these messages and instructions would not be passing back and forth. Still, it probably was not this man. The day operator had only referred to the railroad boss as Tomlin, never once as Walt, so he probably was not as close to Tomlin as were some or all of the others. It was something Longarm intended to keep in mind.

"Thanks for your help," Longarm said.

"Any time."

Longarm made sure the Colt was ready to his hand before he stepped out through the only door of the depot. Someone had been lying in wait for him before. That same someone could be out there again.

No one shot at him this time. He stood beside the door, searching for movement, tense, but he could see nothing but blowing, shifting snow and the pale, empty drifts leading down to the creek below the tracks.

He moved to his right, starting back around the building the way he had come, then paused.

He had gone in that way. Anyone wanting to potshoot him from ambush might be bright enough to let him get out away from shelter and then take him when he waded through the drifts around that end of the building. Better, he thought, to vary his route back, even if it did involve more effort to go the long way around. He turned back and set out along the downwind side of the buried platform.

Three different businessmen in Redcloud confirmed that the accumulation on the Goat Horns was most unusual and a damned dangerous situation.

"I was one of the first in here, mister," a balding store-keeper bragged. The man's sign advertised hardware, but

101

his business seemed to be almost totally devoted to the sale of drill bits and explosives. Kegs of blasting powder, crates of fuse cord labelled by burn rate, and waxed cardboard cartons of blasting caps were piled in orderly confusion throughout the place. "I hope you know better than to light that thing," he said when Longarm pulled a cheroot from his pocket and began to chew on the end of it.

"I know better," Longarm said with a smile.

"Good, 'cause a competitor of mine had him a customer one day that didn't know. Did my trade a world of good, but it's a hard way to get business. Doc Perry's drugstore is built where that store used to be. And wouldn't you know, the asshole that lit his pipe without thinking got blown out the front door and ended up with nothing more wrong than a busted eardrum and his eyebrows singed off." The store-keeper shook his head.

"I just figure to chew it," Longarm said.

The storekeeper nodded. "What was I saying? Oh, yeah. I was one of the very first in here, just after they made the first discoveries. I'd tried my hand at mining, at Tarryall and again at Fairplay, and decided there were better ways to make a living, so when this discovery opened up I was one of the first to come in with supplies for the damn fools who work underground. One of the very first." He nodded again. "And let me tell you, man, I've seen some winters here. Snow ass deep to an elephant. And that's in an *easy* year. Only once before've I seen any snow on the Goat Horns. That was before the railroad came in. An early snow, it was. September, maybe October. Wet like this one and heavy. That time, as I recall, it didn't build up so much as now. Not so much of it between the horns like there is right now. It laid up there slumping for three, four days, maybe. We was all dug out by then, and the mule trail, which is what we had for getting in and out before the railroad built in to us, was open again. Well let me tell you, mister, when that snow turned loose and come a-roaring down the chute, it was damn sure something. Sounded like a tornado or something, and the whole valley was full of snow flung in the air. It was like a whole new storm had come in, there was that much snow thrown from it. Never did know how many men and mules got carried off by it, but there was some bodies turned up downstream come the next spring, and nobody ever will know how many weren't found or washed so far we wouldn't have heard of it. So if you're thinking of trying to get out of here any time soon, well, I'd tell you to stay put. I've seen what a *little* slide off that there mountain can do, and it's more than any human person can imagine. And this one is gonna be worse."

Longarm thanked the man and left. He waited until he was outside again and the hardware store door carefully closed behind him before he lighted the cheroot.

He stood there, still unable to see from one side of the street to the other because of the drifts, although now there were beginning to be some footpaths stamped out across them as people moved back and forth through Redcloud again.

There was no sign of the hidden gunman, nor of Walter Tomlin.

Tomlin's house was way the hell and gone down at the other end of town. It was mid-afternoon now, and Longarm was hungry. The night had been a long one, and breakfast was a long time past. He decided Tomlin's house could wait until after a late lunch.

He drew some of the smoke into his lungs and started across the street toward the nearest cafe.

Chapter 10

The cafe was small and dark and smelled of stale grease and fried onions. At least it was not crowded at this hour between the usual lunch and dinner times. Longarm took a table near the front where he could keep an eye on the street outside the windows, or at least on the near sidewalk. The other side of the street was still invisible beyond the snowdrifts.

A thin, plain girl in a drab, shapeless dress rushed to take his lunch order.

The girl was as drab as her clothing, Longarm thought. Her hair was pulled severely back and wound into an untidy bun. The scuffed toes of heavy work shoes were visible under the tattered hem of her dress. She had thin lips and colorless cheeks. The only spot of color or interest about her would have been her eyes, which were large and wide and a golden hazel shade, but she kept them mostly averted from him as she nervously held a pencil poised over a scrap of paper ready to write down the customer's order. He was practically the only patron in the place, except for a pair of men drinking coffee in a back corner, and she surely should have had no difficulty remembering.

Perhaps she was a bit weak between the ears, Longarm thought. With that in mind he ordered in a slow, clear voice, taking his time about it and trying to be as smilingly pleasant with her as possible.

"Yes, sir." Her voice was sweet and clear, no slurring or hesitation about it, and the pencil tip flew across the bit of paper with quick, sure motions. Possibly she was not simple after all. She certainly was shy and nervous, though. As soon as she had taken the order she turned and literally ran the few steps across the cafe to give the order to a big, sour-looking man standing at the stove. She turned the order in, Longarm noticed, without referring to the paper she still held.

Longarm quit his idle wondering and turned his attention back out to the street. More and more people were braving the wind and the blowing snow to go about their business. Men, and now and then an occasional woman, tramped the footpaths deeper across the drifts.

No one within his range of vision appeared particularly threatening, though, and there was not likely to be any sign of Walter Tomlin. Still, it was only prudent to remain alert. His eyes were on the street, but of course he could hear what was going on inside the cafe.

"I thought I told you to bring in more coal." The voice was that of a man, deep and grating. He managed to give each word a nasty, cutting twist.

"But I did already." That was the girl talking. She sounded frightened and close to tears. "That was the very last that was in the bin. Really."

"This ain't enough for t'night, damn you." The man

was speaking again, angrily, his voice almost to a bellow. "Find some."

There was a moment of silence, then the distinctive slap of flesh striking flesh and a brief squeal of fear and pain.

Longarm snapped his head around in time to see the back of the girl as she ran through a small door into a back room of the cafe. She had a hand pressed to her cheek. The cook, a hairy son of a bitch with belly enough for a pair of pregnant women, was glaring after her.

Longarm frowned. This was none of his business. Exactly. But it pissed him off.

The cook saw Longarm's expression and glared back at him.

If the bastard wanted to make something of this . . .

Longarm tensed and began to rise from his chair. The cook turned quickly away and began to prepare Longarm's meal.

When the food was ready the cook brought it himself. There was no sign of the serving girl. The man carried the plate to Longarm's table and plunked it down in front of him with a clatter, then stalked back to his stove and stood with folded arms and a scowl while Longarm ate mechanically and without pleasure.

Longarm felt no desire to linger here over coffee when he was finished eating. He dropped a coin onto the table, gathered his coat and hat, and left. The meal he had just eaten felt like a lump of warm lead in his stomach, and his mood was not particularly good.

Out on the street the cut of the wind felt clean and almost refreshing after the dark atmosphere of the cafe. He stopped to light another cheroot and thought fleetingly about the bottle of rye in his carpetbag. He would have to pass the hotel anyway on his way to Tomlin's, and he was thinking about stopping in there long enough for a visit to his room.

A small, drab figure rounded one of the drifts in the street and backed into view, dark against the stark white of the snow. It was the girl from the cafe, bent over and facing back the way she had just come. She was dragging a lumpy burlap sack, likely filled with coal, and obviously much too heavy for her to manage. She was trying to sled it across the snow, but she was having trouble with it. Snow kept pushing up in front of the sack and she was not strong enough to lift the coal.

"Well, hell," Longarm said under his breath.

No one else on the street seemed interested in helping her, and he sure could not expect that sourpuss bastard from the cafe to come out and lend a hand. Longarm selected a path that had been tramped into the deep snow and went out to give her a hand.

It did not help his disposition any to realize when he reached her that she was wearing only the thin dress and a ragged shawl that was wrapped around her shoulders. If she owned a proper coat, she had not taken the time to put it on.

"Let me take that," he said gently. He bent to take hold of the wadded mouth of the burlap sacking, and his hand brushed the girl's wrist. Her skin had the chill feel of a corpse's.

Startled by his unexpected appearance, she released her grip on the sack and almost fell backward into the snow. Longarm steadied her, then picked up the sack. It was a heavy son of a bitch, much more than she should have been expected to handle.

"Go on ahead," he said, "before you catch your death out here."

The girl hesitated.

"Go on. Shoo."

She blinked, then turned and ran quickly toward the end of the block of buildings where the cafe was located and out of sight into an alley. The front door of the place was much closer, yet she ran around to the back.

The hell with that, Longarm thought. He had no intention of hauling the sack all the way around to the back door when the front was so near. There must have been a hundredweight of coal in the sack. He hefted it to a balance point high on his back and humped the stuff through the snow to the cafe and inside.

The girl was already inside when he got there. She was shivering and had her arms wrapped tightly around her thin frame. And she was already getting hell from the cook.

"Where the hell—"

"Hold it," Longarm said.

The man turned, his face still contorted with anger.

Longarm carried the sack to him and dropped it at his feet. The mouth of the bag opened, and lumps of hard coal spilled out onto the floor.

"Was there something you were going to say?" Longarm asked mildly.

The cook took a long look at Longarm. The tall deputy's voice had been mild, but there was cold steel in his eyes.

"No," the cook said quickly. His expression moderated just as quickly, shifting from fury to appeasement. "No. I . . . uh, thanks."

"Sure," Longarm said in a flat tone, his eyes still locked on those of the cook.

The cook's eyes shifted nervously away from Longarm's. He swallowed hard and looked down toward the floor. "Was there . . . was there something else I could do for you, mister?"

Longarm hesitated long enough to increase the man's nervousness, then said, "I'll think about that, neighbor. Then we'll see." He paused again. "Won't we?"

"Whatever you say."

"Uh-huh." Longarm turned away and headed toward the door again.

Behind him the girl burst into motion, running to the table Longarm had recently vacated and hurrying to clear it of the dishes Longarm had left there. She had said nothing, he realized, throughout the exchange. Apparently she was too frightened of the cook even to thank Longarm for his help.

He felt sorry for her, but there was nothing else he could do for her without likely making her job all the worse. Besides, he had other things on his mind at the moment. He had forgotten about her before he got to the end of the block.

Longarm pulled his key from his pocket and started to insert it in the lock. He froze there, key in hand, a chill racing up his spine.

Locked or unlocked, someone had been inside the room since he left it early in the morning. Longarm knew damned good and well that he had set the latch when he locked the door and left. That quick pushing, jiggling motion was long since a habit any time he locked a door. Now the door was ajar by a scant fraction of an inch.

Quietly Longarm returned the room key to his pocket and slid the .44-40 Colt into his hand.

He took a half step to the side so that he would not be standing directly in front of the door when it opened, then swiftly raised his right foot and kicked.

The door flew open with a crash as it whipped around and banged into the wall. Before the door was even fully open Longarm was in a crouch and moving forward, the big steel Colt leading the way.

He threw himself forward, rolled, and came back onto his knees far wide of the doorway.

The Colt wound up aimed at a wide-eyed and apparently quite startled—and quite naked—blonde woman.

There was no one else in the room. Longarm made sure of that before he did or thought anything else. There was no one behind the door, no one under the bed, no one hiding inside the tiny wardrobe the management provided. He checked each possible hiding place carefully before he reassured himself by a look at the number on the door that he was indeed in the correct room. Then he closed and locked the door behind him. Only then did he take the time to pay attention to the woman who was reclining, much more at ease now, on his bed.

Longarm touched the brim of his Stetson in a gesture that mocked a gentleman's customary greeting to a lady. "Miss Emma. Nice to see you."

Emma gave him a smile of wry amusement, possibly at the precautions against ambush he had just taken, and then stretched with a slow, sinuous grace.

Naked, she looked as sleek and glossy as a mountain cat. She was, he had to admit, quite an eyeful. Long, well-formed legs, slim thighs melting delightfully into a rounded swell of hip. Flat belly underscored by a patch of pale curling pubic hair. Firm, pink-tipped breasts. And, of course, that incredibly lovely face. She still wore her cameo earrings, but nothing else except that faint smile.

Oddly, his eyes were drawn again and again to the

molded perfection of her throat, so very slender and vulnerable. He could see her pulse beating in the hollow at the base of it. He licked suddenly dry lips and felt a surge of response to her.

Emma's gaze dropped to a point slightly below Longarm's belt, and her smile became wider. She rolled onto her side with a fluid, languorous motion and propped herself up on her elbow.

Slowly and with deliberate provocation she fixed her stare on the bulge in Longarm's corduroys and ran the pink tip of her tongue over full and already moist lips. She gave a little wiggle and let her eyelids droop closed.

Longarm knew damned good and well that this whole thing was a fake. It had to be. She had told him herself that she played only for pay, and top wages at that. But, *damn*, she was something.

A thrill of anticipation ran through him as the beautiful woman let her head loll back onto his pillow, her eyes still closed.

It had only been seconds, and already he was beginning to ache from wanting her. He shuddered, another chill dancing the length of his spine, and forced himself to think about more important things.

The door was closed and now bolted from the inside. No one was going to come through it without warning. There was no balcony outside the hotel-room window. He checked the window anyway. It was closed against the icy thrust of the wind. He made sure it was locked, then drew the shade down so that no one outside could see to shoot at him through the glass.

What did the woman want here? Apart from the obvious. He did not believe that for a moment.

Emma opened her eyes, smiled at him, and patted the

111

edge of the bed. "Sit here, Longarm. Where I can touch you." She licked her lips again. "Where you can touch me."

Longarm went to her side, but it was not Emma he touched. He did his best to ignore her while he snatched the pillow from under her head and checked under it, then inside the pillowcase, for a hidden derringer or knife or cudgel. There was nothing. Emma gave him a curious look. Then she began to laugh.

He threw the covers back off the bed and checked there too, then around the rim of the bed between the mattress and the creaky springs. Finally he found her handbag on the nightstand and inspected it for weapons. There was nothing.

"Satisfied, dear?" she asked in a tone of lazy contentment.

"No," he said. "What are you doing here?"

"Isn't that obvious, darling? I've been thinking about you since your visit this morning." With another slow, cat-like smile she ran her fingertips lightly down his chest to his belt and below it, finding and fondling him there with quick, gentle skill.

"After all," she said, "even a working girl likes to have fun." She laughed. "Sometimes." She squeezed him.

Longarm felt a surge of heat race through his blood. She was so very damned desirable, so lovely.

She leaned forward, parted those full lips, and pressed her face against him, covering him with her open mouth through the cloth that bound him.

She breathed out slowly, and Longarm could feel the heat of her breath penetrate the cloth to touch and surround the sensitive skin.

She withdrew her mouth and once again began to stroke him through the cloth. "You're big," she whispered. "So big. I hoped you would be, you know. To match those gorgeous muscles." Again she applied her mouth to him through the corduroy barrier while her hand played across his chest and stomach.

"Come to me," she whispered. "Let me show you everything I know." Her eyelids drooped shut again as if in anticipation of the delights they would share. "Everything," she whispered. "Everything."

The heat of her breath surrounded him once more as she pressed her open lips against his bulge.

He felt his knees weaken and buckle. He very nearly fell on top of her. He reached down to steady himself, and his groping hand encountered the smooth curve of her right breast. It was softer than he would have expected. Her flesh flowed between his fingers like warm butter.

Emma laughed and turned herself to him so that he could touch her. She was unbelievably beautiful, skilled, and willing.

Longarm's mouth went dry. He swallowed with some difficulty. Then, with a growl of displeasure, he tore himself away from her searching, groping, grasping touch.

He turned his back on the exquisite Miss Emma and stalked out of the hotel room, the revolver already in his hand even as he slammed the door loudly shut behind him.

Chapter 11

Longarm took the stairs at a dead run, charged through the lobby, and burst outside into the cold, swirling wind with his gun held ready.

He turned to his right and ran the length of the Redcloud business street, past the railroad depot across the way, and down to Tomlin's house.

He fully expected to find Walter Tomlin out in the open and likely wearing snowshoes, making a break for freedom in spite of the dangers from up on the Goat Horns.

Emma had told him herself that she played only for the pay. *Someone had damn sure paid her to distract him.*

And he wasn't buying. Not her, not the distraction she presented. No matter how desirable she was.

A slight ache hanging low in his groin painfully reminded him just how desirable the woman was. But he was not going to let Tomlin get away for the sake of *any* woman.

He lumbered to a halt in front of Tomlin's house, his chest heaving as the cold air bit hard and deep in his laboring lungs.

From there he could see the rolling, drifted field of snow that covered the railroad tracks and ran from the depot down into the narrow canyon that led to Silverton and civilization. It was unblemished snow, virgin and new-fallen, unmarked by the deep, distinctive herring-bone tracks of a set of snowshoes.

The wind was still strong, but not hard enough now to wipe out tracks immediately. that would take some little time anyway, and Longarm had not been in the hotel room with Emma nearly long enough.

No one had tried to leave Redcloud. Not yet.

He shoved his Colt back into its holster and buttoned his coat closed. He had not taken time to do that in his rush to get out of the hotel, and he was becoming cold.

Above him and to his right he heard some chuckling and then a few catcalls.

A group of men he recognized as railroad employees came out of Tomlin's door to stand on their missing boss's porch and jeer at the deputy standing below them. Longarm flexed the chilled fingers of his right hand, ready to drag iron again if any of the men wanted to offer trouble. After all, someone, very possibly one of these men, had already taken one shot at him. Longarm did not intend to welcome a second opportunity for the gunman.

Thoroughly furious now, Longarm climbed the steps to the front of Tomlin's house. Someone had gone to the trouble of sweeping the stairs clear not long before.

The railroaders on the porch—there were five of them —were smirking.

"What's so funny?" Longarm demanded.

"Oh, just a bet we were having," Franklin Jewett said.

115

Jewett was the only one of them whose name Longarm could recall at the moment.

"About . . . ?"

Jewett grinned. "About whether you'd fall for it," the man admitted with pleasure. "I said you wouldn't." He hooked a thumb toward a thin, bearded man who Longarm thought was one of the brakemen on the stranded relief crew. "Tommy said you'd stay in that hotel room getting your ashes hauled an' never give a thought to anything else."

"And what did Tomlin say?"

Jewett grinned again. "Walt didn't expect you to go for it any more than I did. But he figured it was worth a try."

Longarm made a sour face. If he had only thought quickly enough he would have stayed in that room a little longer, long enough to convince these grinning pricks that he had fallen for their little joke. Tomlin just might have come out into the open, might have tried to make his run, avalanche threat or no, if Longarm had done that.

Not now, though. Now the man was spooked for sure. There was no way he would be trying it now.

On the other hand, Longarm realized, this little display could well have a flip side to it. Tomlin would be doubly cautious now about trying to venture out. Wherever the bastard was, he was likely to stay there. That was something.

"You boys are gonna have to clear this house now," Longarm said.

"What?"

"You heard me. The party's over. I'm closing this place. Preservation of evidence for federal offenses. So clear out, all of you, and don't come back."

The giggles and grins disappeared. They seemed to

116

think they were all entitled to open-house fun at good old Walt's.

One of them, the brakeman Jewett had called Tommy, grumbled, "The sheriff said you didn't have no authority here."

Longarm fixed the man with a stare that was considerably colder than the bone-chilling temperature out on the porch. "I don't care what your bourbon-for-brains sheriff said, mister. This is a federal matter, and I do intend to enforce federal law on it. If you want to discuss the fine points of law with a judge I'll be glad to accommodate any of you, and put you in cuffs until I can get you to the nearest federal judge. Would you like me to do that?"

The man turned his face away and said nothing.

"Tomlin hasn't done you any of you any favors by letting you get mixed into this. Now get out of here before I start making arrests just to make me feel better."

The men did not look happy about it, but they moved. Longarm followed them back inside the house while they gathered up their things, then trailed them to the door.

When the last of them was gone he sighed. He surely was becoming a popular son of a bitch in Redcloud lately.

He turned and found the door leading down to Tomlin's basement. It was time he gave the place a thorough searching.

Just because Walter Tomlin's house was too obvious a place for a man to hide, that did not mean Tomlin would not hide out there. After all, sometimes the very best place to hide something was in plain sight.

He started in the basement and worked his way up, room by room and cranny by cranny, to and including the dustiest corners of Tomlin's attic.

He found nothing, but he did not consider the time to

117

have been wasted. At least he knew of another place in Redcloud where Walter Tomlin *wasn't* hiding.

The hotel room was empty save for its sparse furnishings, the cot that had been set up in the corner for the now absent Tomlin, and Longarm's few personal possessions. There was no sign of Emma. *Damn her,* Longarm thought with gritted teeth. He could remember all too clearly the sight and the feel of her, the sleek, luxurious beauty that could tease a man almost beyond reason.

Oh, he could remember her, all right, but not fondly. Not knowing what she had tried to do there. Especially after discovering that when she dressed and left she left the door to his room standing wide open so that any son of a bitch with a yen for easy pickings could have come in and pilfered Longarm's belongings.

Even so, his mouth went dry and his pecker throbbed at the remembered look and touch of her.

He closed the door behind him and took several minutes to go through his carpetbag, making sure nothing had been stolen while he was away. Then, far more important, he unloaded the Winchester that had been left in its scabbard and satisfied himself that no one had fiddled with it while he was out. The action worked as it should, and the blunt-nosed cartridges appeared to be undamaged. With a grunt of continued annoyance, Longarm replaced everything as it had been and took a short nip from his bottle of rye. The liquor warmed him but did nothing for his disposition. The glaring emptiness of the hotel room, with neither his prisoner nor that bitch in it, emphasized his foul humor. Better to leave the reminder behind him, he decided.

He closed and carefully locked the door, then placed a few telltales around the jamb so he would know if anyone had been in—again—while he was absent. Then he headed down into the lobby.

It was coming evening, and the hotel restaurant was full and much noisier than Longarm felt like putting up with at the moment. He buttoned his coat, pulled his gloves on, and drifted out into the street.

The wind had picked up again, cutting through and beneath protective clothing. It would have been a bitch of a night to spend outdoors. There was still enough light that he could see a plume of white blowing off the Goat Horns where uncounted tons of snow lay ready to bury the unwary. Many of the people he could see on the street were casting nervous glances toward the crag and the coming avalanche. They knew it had to come down and they dreaded it, even though they were trapped here until its power was expended. At least the path it had to follow would run wide of the town.

Longarm shrugged deeper into the collar of his coat and followed the sidewalk up the street.

He was not really hungry yet after the late lunch he had had, but a cup of coffee would be welcome. He turned into the greasy cafe where he had eaten earlier. The lamps had been lighted inside the place, and it was brighter and more pleasant-seeming now, in the dim light of dusk, than it had been in mid-afternoon.

The same man was doing the cooking, and the same harried girl was trying to wait on the busy tables. Longarm found a spot at a not quite full table and sat, relishing the warmth put off by the stove in the back corner where the cook was busy burning meat.

"Yes, sir?" the girl asked as she rushed to take his order. She stood with pad and pencil poised and no recognition apparent on her face, but in a furtive whisper, her lips barely moving, she added, "Thank you, sir."

Longarm glanced from her to the cook. The pot-bellied man was scowling toward them. When he saw Longarm look in his direction he turned his face away.

"Just coffee, please."

"Yes, sir." She dutifully wrote down the simple order, paused for only a fraction of a second to give him a helpless look of gratitude, and then hurried away.

A man to Longarm's left started to say something, but Longarm's attention was diverted when the cook turned to the girl and snapped, "You! I'm running short here. Fetch in 'nother quarter of meat."

The girl bobbed her head and hurried into the back of the place. She was back within seconds, her hands empty. "There isn't another," Longarm heard her say. She looked frightened, as if she would be blamed for the lack.

"What?" the big man bellowed. He raised a hand as if to strike her. Then he tensed. He might well have been remembering the tall, lean, extremely stern man who was watching at his back. Instead the cook hissed something at her under his breath and disappeared into the back room. He was back within seconds also, and his hands were also empty.

"Go get the sheriff," he snapped. "Some son of a bitch has robbed me of my last quarter o' beef."

The girl bobbed her head quickly and disappeared through the back door.

"Oh, shit," the man at Longarm's left said. Apparently his attention had been drawn to the brief exchange by Longarm's concentration on it.

"What's the trouble?" Longarm asked him.

"You ever been in a stranded camp before, mister?" the man asked.

Longarm shook his head.

"I have. Once. In Bailey, it was. Bad joss, I'll tell you." The man took a swallow of his coffee, reminding Longarm that his own coffee had not yet been delivered and likely would not be for some time now.

"It was a bitch of a hard winter, that one," the man continued. "No railroads with plows back then, you see. We got snowbound that year." He nodded grimly. "Bad. Men turned into a bunch of fuckin' animals, let me tell you. Quick as we knew what was up, *every* damn thing disappeared. Food, liquor, candles, even soap. Folks hoarded whatever they had an' stole whatever they could. Loaf o' bread was worth a man's life, that time. Wasn't no such thing as sharing, neither, for we hadn't any idea when any of us would get out of it. An' some of them boys didn't get out of it. Couple o' fellows actually starved to death while others thirty, forty yards away was holed up in cabins with root cellars piled full o' supplies. But they wouldn't share none of it. Not even to save a man's life. And those that didn't starve . . . well, some didn't make it for the lead and the steel that was used to protect whatever one man had from anybody else that came near. Bad joss," the man said again. "I hope to hell that don't happen here."

"You survived it," Longarm pointed out.

"Aye, I did. Me and my partners made it through. An' what's more, I'll survive this one too. I know what t' do before the fever gets onto everybody." Quickly the man stood, taking a moment to scoop some leftover rolls into his coat pockets. He hurried out of the cafe without remembering to pay for his meal.

Longarm sat in stunned surprise. In the few moments they had been talking, the friendly, open-faced miner had undergone a transformation into a stern, worried man with the harsh look of greed on his features.

"Lordy," Longarm muttered to himself.

The serving girl returned, through the front door this time, with a wobbly, slack-jawed sheriff in tow. As before, she was wearing only the thin dress and the entirely inadequate shawl, even though the evening temperatures would be even lower now that the thin sunlight had disappeared.

"What sheems t' be the problem here?" Maxwell asked in a loud, thick voice.

"Some son of a bitch broke into my back room an' stole half a beef," the cook reported. Longarm noted that the amount of meat stolen had suddenly risen from a quarter to a half, but he said nothing. Maxwell had not yet noticed the federal deputy among the cafe's customers, and Longarm figured the evening probably would be more pleasant if that state of affairs continued.

The sheriff scowled and hitched up his belt, his fingers playing along the side of it absently as if searching for a holster or weapon that was not there. "That's serious, Don."

"Damn right it's serious," the cook agreed. "I got a delivery due on the next train, but what the hell am I supposed to feed m' customers until then?"

Maxwell grunted something Longarm could not hear and went into the back room where the missing beef was supposed to have been. The cook followed him.

The girl, still shivering, wrapped her shawl closer around her thin shoulders and began trying to wait on the tables once more. She remembered at last to bring Longarm his coffee.

Chapter 12

Spreading word about the stolen beef was like the lifting of a floodgate. Within three quarters of an hour the residents of Redcloud were flooding the street and the stores, their expressions hard and their jaws set, a look of glassy determination in their eyes. They were not panicked—not yet —but they were close to it. They carried the last pennies of their savings in white-knuckled fists and tried to buy up anything and everything they could find, almost without regard for any given article's value.

Men who already wore garments heavy enough to carry them through two winters without shelter offered outrageous sums for woolen scarves by the dozen. The price of a tin of beef biscuit quadrupled to begin with and then soared upward from there.

Longarm was in a saloon having a quiet drink when it started. His first indication of what was happening was when four men dashed inside, slapped their gold onto the bar, and ordered whiskey by the case, all of it that their money would buy.

Other men who had already been at the bar looked at them with amused curiosity at first, then with suspicion. Whispered rumors began quickly to circulate through the smoky room. Then they too began to demand bottles or cases of liquor instead of drinks by the glass. Within fifteen minutes the bartender had completely sold out his stock on hand and had only kegs of beer remaining for his customers. Some of the men were even trying to buy those.

Longarm could see the anguish cross the bartender's face when the man belatedly realized that he could have commanded a price for his whiskey even greater than he had. And the price had been steadily rising during those last few minutes, as anxious customers shouted higher and higher offers for the dwindling number of bottles available.

Longarm finished the drink he had in front of him. It looked like that one and whatever he had remaining in his hotel room were going to have to see him through until the Goat Horns shed their skin and the train bulled its way in. He went outside to see what was happening elsewhere in the town.

The long main street was an anthill of activity, cold and wind and darkness notwithstanding. Men ran from one place to the next with pokes of money in their hands. Some clutched purchases already made tight against their chests and dashed for safety with their shoulders hunched and expressions grim, fearful of strongarm theft before they might get their store of goods hoarded and hidden.

In the next block a storekeeper had his doors locked and his shop closed. He was inside, refusing to reopen after hours. A crowd gathered in front of the bolted door, shouting threats if the man did not open up and sell to them.

One fool in the crowd actually managed to find a torch

124

somewhere and threatened to set fire to the business if the shopkeeper did not open his doors to them. The torch guttered and flared, yellow and smoky in the grip of the wind, and was extinguished by the gale before any damage was done.

Longarm shook his head in a mixture of sadness and disbelief. Whatever supplies the storekeeper might have inside that building, burning them was not likely to accomplish a whole hell of a lot. The quickly panicking miners did not seem to be thinking about that, though. They only wanted their hands on everything they could grab right now. Tomorrow they might need it.

The tall deputy jammed the stub of a half-smoked cheroot between his teeth and took a step forward. This was not a federal matter, was part of no jurisdiction that he could reasonably claim, but he could not stand and watch while a bunch of idiots broke into someone's place of business.

Before Longarm could reach the group Sheriff Evan Maxwell joined them, pushing his way into the crowd from the other direction, and shoved his way forward until he was standing in front of the men with his back to the closed door.

Maxwell had been in bad shape when Longarm saw him at the cafe a little while earlier, but he looked almost sober now, likely shocked into a degree of sobriety by what he was seeing in his town. He swayed only once, caught himself against the door at his back, and made an effort to stand upright with his shoulders squared.

"Settle down, damn it!" the sheriff roared. There was a sharp snap of authority in his voice, and for the first time Longarm could get some hint of what kind of lawman the sheriff might once have been.

The yammering of the crowd lessened, and for a

moment even died away. For a moment Longarm thought the old boy was going to be able to handle it. That moment did not last long. Past reputation and old authority could not hope to compete with the stumbling drunk these miners saw in their sheriff day in and day out. The brief hesitation of the crowd was broken by a voice from somewhere in the pack. "Fuck off, you old bastard."

Someone else grabbed Maxwell's arm and jerked at him. The sheriff lost his balance and went to his knees. The mob-like roaring of the crowd returned, and again they were shouting for the storekeeper to open his doors.

Men at the back of the crowd searched on the ground for missiles to throw, found nothing except the thick blanket of snow that covered the street, and made do by packing huge snowballs and pelting the storefront with those. Glass in the streetside windows shattered and fell to the sidewalk.

Longarm elbowed his way through the frightened men. And that was what they were, he realized: frightened. Scared beyond reason by the thought of being isolated here without food enough to carry them through until the relief train arrived. He shoved his way to the front and bent to take Maxwell by the arm and help the sheriff to his feet. Maxwell looked confused, probably still muddled by the liquor in his system, but he made an effort to pull himself together again and to stand in front of the mob with some degree of dignity and resolution.

"Quiet!" the sheriff barked.

He was ignored. One of the men stepped forward and began knocking out the still unbroken panes of glass from the shopkeeper's windows. None of the men in the crowd seemed in the least interested in sweet reason.

Longarm drew the big Thunderer and triggered a shot into the air over the heads of the miners. The bellow of the

Colt cut through the noise of the crowd and stopped it with the suddenness of a snapping string.

Heads turned and wide eyes sought to focus on the lean deputy and on the small, graying drunk at his side.

Maxwell looked at Longarm too but he did not seem as belligerent now as he had the last time they had spoken. Now he looked grateful.

Longarm nodded for Maxwell to take over now. He took a half step backward, deferring to the sheriff's local authority.

Maxwell gave him a brief look of gratitude and turned to face the crowd. "Off the street, all you you." He paused, clenching his jaw tight shut to contain a belch that was trying to force its way through his throat, then continued. "I'm ordering all stores closed." He blinked and for a moment Longarm thought he was going to ruin the whole thing by staggering sideways, but he caught himself in time. "All of them until further notice," Maxwell said in a strong, clear voice.

"There is no emergency here. *No* emergency." He closed his mouth to hide another belch. "If an emergency arises I will . . . uh, I will declare martial law in this town."

A man near the front of the crowd opened his mouth to jeer at the little sheriff.

"If Sheriff Maxwell enters a request for martial law in Redcloud," Longarm said before anyone else could pick up on the hooting, "I will help him enforce it."

"So who the hell are you, mister?" someone in the crowd shouted.

"Federal officer," Longarm said quietly. He still had the big Colt in his right hand. He used his left to pull out his wallet and flip it open so the men could see the gleam of his badge in the light of their lanterns. The faces he could see in front of him became more serious.

"Go home now," Longarm said. "We'll tell you in the morning if the stores can reopen. If necessary, we will assemble all the food in town at one central point and start a rationing program. No one here will go hungry while others are eating. No one."

"No one," Maxwell repeated. His voice was strong now and he seemed to have good control of himself.

There was some muttering among the men in the crowd, but they were no longer acting like a mob. They were a group of individuals, frightened and unsure. And more than likely they were ashamed as well, Longarm suspected.

One by one, men began to turn and slip silently away until only a last few diehards were left. Then they too ducked their eyes away from Longarm's and went off into the night.

Behind him, inside the store, Longarm could hear the shopkeeper moving about and clattering something solid behind the shutters that covered his broken windows. The man never had opened his door and did not offer to do so now.

"We'd better start enforcing that shut-down order of yours," Longarm said to Maxwell. "I'd suggest you leave the saloons and the whorehouses open, but it's up to you."

Maxwell blinked and shivered, but he was more sober now than he likely had been for months past. He nodded once and led the way up the street.

"Like hell you will." The man had looked worried before. Now he was furious. He was a customer in the store, not the proprietor. Oddly enough—or perhaps not so strangely, since prices might be expected to go even higher tomorrow—Longarm and Maxwell had received little complaint from the storekeepers when the shut-down instructions were given. For the most part, the storekeepers were more than willing to see their frantic customers chased outside and their doors locked.

"I been in line here for an *hour*," the thwarted customer complained loudly. "Now you come in an' tell Johnson to close an' only *two* people in front o' me? Like shit you do."

Johnson, the owner of this particular place, seemed to be one who likely did not really need to be closed down, Longarm realized. The man had his customers organized into a neat, orderly queue. There was no shoving, no shouting, no bullying toward the front here. Apparently there was no impromptu auction either, where a given piece of merchandise would be awarded to the miner or miners offering the highest bids from among a half-panicked crowd.

Judging from the relatively light burdens he had seen in the arms of men leaving the store, too, Longarm guessed that Johnson had already instituted a sort of rationing, limiting the purchases of his customers so as to make sure that there would be something left for those who came later.

Johnson had actually looked relieved when Maxwell announced his order for the stores to be closed.

"Sorry," Longarm said to the angry miner. "No exceptions."

"But you don't understand, man," the miner wailed. "I got me a woman at home. She's expectin', man. I can't let her go without somethin' to eat."

Longarm gave the frightened man a calming smile. "Do you have enough in the house for tonight and tomorrow morning's breakfast?"

"Well, sure, but—"

"We won't let her go hungry. Or you either. That's the whole point of this. We don't intend for anyone to go hungry. There will be food enough for everyone. *If* we don't let a few grab off all the food there is in town and hide it away from those who are hungry. You see?" Longarm was still smiling, his voice gentle and soothing.

The miner's face twisted with anguish. That lasted for only a moment. Then his eyes shifted away from Longarm's, and he got a crafty, furtive look about him. He nodded, and pretended a phony-looking smile. He made as if to turn away from the counter he had been so close to.

Then, with much more warning than he realized, he turned and grabbed blindly toward the burlap sack of goods placed on the counter for the customer Johnson had been waiting on there.

He snatched up the sack and dashed toward the door. He took the sack in his left hand and with his right produced a showy but almost uselessly large Bowie knife that he had had hidden under his coat, probably stuck down behind his belt without benefit of a sheath or scabbard.

The men who had been behind him in the line jumped out of his way as the thoroughly panicked miner slashed the wicked knife blade in wide sweeps before him as he ran.

With a muttered "Shit," Longarm stepped in front of the charging man.

The fellow stopped, but only for a moment. There were tears of frustration bringing an unnatural brightness to his eyes, and he clutched the sack of foodstuffs to his chest protectively.

"I got . . . I just got to . . ." He was breathing in quick, ragged gasps. He was scared of what he had already done, and of what he intended still to do. But he was determined too. His concern for the well-being of his wife was greater

130

than his fear of Longarm or of any other lawman. Or of any ethical considerations whatsoever. In his unthinking panic, he knew only that he *had* to take food home to hoard away against uncertain need.

With a squeal, the man charged forward, swinging the heavy blade in front of him, chopping it wickedly toward Longarm's throat.

Longarm had every right to shoot the man down in self-defense. It would have been the safe course for him to take. The .44-40 Colt had long since been ready in his hand. He did not bother to take the time even to consider it.

Instead of shooting the man or ducking prudently out of his way, Longarm timed the man's blind charge and then stepped forward, into the face of the charge and the swinging knife, to meet the assault.

His left forearm swept up to flick harmlessly overhead the chopping slash that had been aimed at his throat.

He raised the big Colt, its muzzle pointed toward the ceiling, and the flat of the butt descended with a blur of speed to strike the frightened miner over his right temple.

The man's eyes rolled back in his head. Both the knife and the sack of food dropped from suddenly nerveless fingers, and with a groan he collapsed forward to his knees. He wavered there for a moment, then toppled the rest of the way, ending face down and totally unconscious on the floor of the store.

"Jesus," someone whispered.

Longarm picked up the sack and handed it to the man who had just bought and paid for the items. The fellow accepted the bundle wordlessly and hurried out of the store.

The other men who had been in line seemed inclined to linger behind.

131

"Do any of you know this man?" Longarm asked.

Nearly all of them nodded.

"Do you know where he lives?"

About half nodded this time.

"You and you," Longarm said, pointing, "I'd appreciate it if you men would take him home to his missus. She'll be wondering where he is."

"You ain't gonna arrest him?" someone asked.

Longarm shook his head. "We'll let it go at the headache he'll be having for the next couple days. He was just scared." Longarm glanced down toward the sheriff, who had not said anything or made a motion since his announcement of the closing order. "Unless Sheriff Maxwell objects, that is."

"Huh? Oh." Maxwell shook his head.

The two men Longarm had designated bent to haul the still unconscious miner upright, and the others began to file quietly out of the store.

"You sure put the poor sumbitch out," someone observed.

"Funny way you buffaloed him, though," another man said. "I seen boys get their heads split open before, but the coppers most gen'rly pistol-whip 'em. How come you done it with the butt like that?"

Longarm winked at Maxwell and nudged the graying man with his elbow. Instead of answering the question himself he passed it on, hoping Maxwell once had been a good enough lawman to know the answer, and that the Redcloud sheriff was not so fuzzy-minded from months or years of drink that he would be unable to remember. It would be a good chance for Maxwell to begin reestablishing a beginning of respect in the town.

"I'll bet your sheriff can tell you," Longarm drawled.

Maxwell looked up at Longarm and blinked. For a

moment Longarm wondered if the sheriff had been paying attention to the question. By now the men still in the store seemed genuinely interested in the answer. Those who had not yet left paused and waited.

Maxwell blinked again, then turned toward the men whose safety he was charged to protect. The aging sot affected a slight swagger and managed a look of smugness.

"That's pretty simple, boys," Maxwell said. "Only an asshole hits something with the barrel of his revolver. Bend the son of a bitch that way, you will. You see somebody buffalo a boy with the barrel end of his shooter, why, he don't know nothing about shooting. This youngster here . . ." He hooked a thumb toward Longarm. "He knows what's what. Does things right, he does. Why, in near thirty years of wearing a badge, I never once hit anyone with the barrel of my pistol."

Maxwell was warming to the idea of having someone actually listen to him. That had probably been rare in recent times. "Why, I could tell you boys something about the way this here job oughta be done. In fact, there was this one time, down in Arizona Territory it was . . ."

The men who had been interested in hearing the explanation quickly found that they had other, urgent things to do elsewhere. They began to mutter excuses among themselves and to head for the door.

Longarm was pleased, though, to realize that at least several of them went to the bother of throwing explanations of their departure over their shoulders for the benefit of the sheriff as they were heading out the door. He doubted that many of them would have bothered if the sheriff had been in his usual wobbly condition.

Longarm glanced toward Maxwell again. The sheriff was still talking, rattling off some antique windy from the dim and distant past, apparently oblivious to the fact that his audience was down to just Longarm and the store-keeper, Johnson.

Longarm winked at Johnson and led the talkative sheriff outside. He was sure Maxwell's tale was a fascinating one and one he would benefit from hearing. But right now they had other places to visit if the hoarding panic was to be stopped before it went too far.

Chapter 13

Longarm deposited the sheriff back at the jail, which also seemed to serve as the man's living quarters. How anyone could stand to live in such depressing surroundings was beyond Longarm's understanding. Still, if a man was drunk enough . . .

Maxwell had been sobered by the evening's activities, and he said nothing about jumping back into a bottle. Whether he would do so again once the federal deputy was out of sight was another matter. Longarm would prefer for the Redcloud sheriff to remain sober, but that would be up to Maxwell and his own sense of duty. Longarm could not hope to keep Maxwell away from liquor if the man really wanted to go back to the booze. That was a lesson Longarm had learned in the past from other drunks. Furthermore, no one had given Evan Maxwell to Custis Long to raise. Longarm had his own problems.

"Good night, Sheriff," Longarm said politely. The

man's unreasoned hatred of the federal deputy seemed to have been suspended for the evening, and Longarm's expression was polite, his tone deliberately respectful.

"You'll help me again in the morning?" Maxwell asked hopefully.

"Of course."

"Good. Good." Maxwell turned away and began to rummage in a desk drawer.

Longarm left the shabby jail. Through the front window he could see Maxwell remove a dark brown pint bottle from his desk and set it among the litter that covered the desktop. Shaking his head, Longarm headed back toward the hotel. It was cold, it was late, and he was hungry. At least there was no more snow falling to add to the discomforts of the night.

He hunched deeper into the sheepskin collar lining of his coat and increased his pace.

As he moved lightly down off a sidewalk section to cross the mouth of an alley separating two of Redcloud's building blocks, he was aware of movement to his left, at the far end of the alley. He might have been tired, but his senses were still sharply attuned after the gunshot that had been thrown his way earlier.

He whirled, dropping into a crouch, his hand sweeping the Colt from its holster under his coat almost before he had time to register the fact of the movement consciously. The barrel of the revolver lined up on the dimly seen form that was perhaps forty feet away.

A high-pitched voice let out a short yelp of fear. He could see now the spread of skirts and a mass of hair on the hatless figure. The person dropped whatever she had been holding.

"Damn," Longarm said under his breath. "I'm sorry,"

he said more loudly, so the woman could hear. "I didn't mean to frighten you."

He moved toward her to apologize further, but he kept the revolver in his hand. It was, after all, not inconceivable that Walter Tomlin's friends could again use a woman to try to sucker him.

"Why, you're the girl from the cafe," Longarm said as he came closer. There was little light at the back of the alley, but some lamplight spilled out of nearby windows, enough to let him recognize the girl when he was near her.

"I wasn't doing nothing wrong, mister. I swear I wasn't," she said hastily. She looked frightened in spite of his apology.

She looked damn well cold. As before, she was wearing only the thin cotton dress she had been working in and the entirely inadequate shawl. At her feet, lying in the banked snow that had fallen into the gap between the store building and the mountainside at its rear, he could see the article she had dropped when he had startled her. It was a grease-stained rag. A bundle of other, equally filthy rags had been placed on top of a broken barrel nearby. Surely she had not . . .

"What are you doing?" he asked in a gentle voice.

"Nothing wrong, mister. I swear that's true. This stuff was trash. It isn't wrong to pick trash, is it?" She pointed vaguely toward the bundle of rags.

"No, of course not, but what did you want with that stuff?"

She shrugged, shivering. "I just . . . I was just gonna see if I couldn't sew some of those together. Or pin them or something."

"Why?"

For the first time a touch of anger flashed in her eyes.

137

"'Cause I'm cold, damn it. A fine gentleman like you might not know what it's like to be cold an' poor, I expect, but that's what I'm doing. I'm looking for some way to stay warm."

"With those?"

"With any damn thing, mister."

"But . . . where do you live?"

"Noplace now." She sniffed. He thought it was more from anger than from a cold. "That son of a bitch Don got to worrying about me eating up his supplies, so he kicked me out. Used to be I slept there in the cafe after he closed up. Now I got noplace."

Longarm sighed and looked around. Seeing nothing that looked suspicious, he shoved the Colt back under his coat. Apparently the hoarding fever extended beyond the miners to those who should have had no worries about it at all. Not that Longarm's opinion of Don had been all that high to begin with.

"Well, it isn't decent for you to be out picking trash in the alleys on a night like this." He hesitated only for a moment, then decided the hell with propriety. This was not exactly a normal situation. "There's a spare cot in my room that isn't being used. It isn't much, but it's warm. Come morning, maybe we can promote you a coat or something."

She looked at him closely for a moment, then nodded. "I already owe you for helping me this afternoon. I'd appreciate this too."

"All right, then."

She started to gather up her bundle of rags.

"You can leave those," he said. "You won't be needing them now."

She gave him a questioning look and, rather than abandon the fruits of her labors, stashed them inside a broken barrel where she could come back to them if necessary.

Only then was she willing to leave them behind and follow Longarm to the hotel.

The hotel was warm enough inside, although the lobby was dimly lighted. Few of the lamps were burning, even though the hour was not that greatly advanced. The attached restaurant was closed for the night.

When Longarm asked if he could get a late meal sent up to his room, the clerk—a friend of Walter Tomlin, Longarm recalled—gave him a smug look of refusal.

"In case you haven't heard, Marshal," the desk man said, "we're cutting back on things. Whole town, practically, is closed up. Cutting back on everything. That's why we aren't using so many lamps. And in half an hour we'll quit firing the boiler too. Got to save on coal and oil and such, you know." The man's expression indicated that he would be positively pleased if the deputy's night was an uncomfortable one.

Longarm grunted and turned toward the stairs, the girl following close behind him.

"Hold it," the clerk said sharply.

"Yes?"

"You can't take no hoor up to the room here. We run a respectable place."

Longarm gave the man a look that was as cold as the weather beyond the front door. "You do like to push, don't you?"

"Just abiding by the rules," the man said primly.

"You do that, mister, but I suggest you do it without insulting decent ladies."

"Decent?" The clerk gave the girl a hard look.

Longarm nodded slowly. "That's what I said. Decent. Do you want to argue about it?"

The clerk took a closer look at Longarm's expression and backed off. "No, I . . . uh, I reckon not."

"Good."

"Two in a room, though . . ."

"You're already charging me for that cot," Longarm snapped. "Or do you want to argue about that too?"

"Uh, no."

Longarm took the nervous-looking girl by the arm and led her up to his room.

He checked the telltales he had left along the edge of the door. No one had been inside since he had left unless they had come in through the window. Even so he took no chances. The girl gave him some questioning looks but said nothing until they were both inside.

When the door was locked and bolted behind them and the window checked to make sure it had not been prised open, she did not even take the time to wrap herself in a blanket and warm up before she said something in a soft whisper that he thought was, "All right, then."

Longarm was busy hanging his coat in the wardrobe and arranging the buckled gunbelt on the bedpost to suit him. He turned and looked at her.

She had already tossed her shawl on the foot of the cot and had kicked off her shoes. She was in the process of getting out of her dress too, shucking the dress and a tattered pair of cotton drawers in one motion. She was wearing nothing else.

She was really quite a pathetic little thing, thin and bony. Her eyes, her lone good feature, were downcast and turned shamefaced away from his. In spite of the determination to carry through with this that he could see in the set of her jaw, when she realized he had turned toward her she turned partially away from him as if with shame.

He could see then that her back, painfully thin as was the rest of her wasted frame, was a latticework of bruises, some obviously fresh and some a fading purple of older

140

abuses. Someone had caned her, and more than once.

"What the hell are you doing?" he blurted.

"I got . . . I mean, I thought . . ." Her cheeks flushed with color.

Longarm crossed over to her and gently pulled the dress back up to drape it loosely over her shoulders. He pulled the material closed at her throat to cover her bare chest and lightly stroked her cheek.

"You don't have any debts to pay," he said softly. "Not here. All I'm wanting is for you to be warm and comfortable tonight. And come morning we'll see about getting both of us fed. Nothing more than that."

The girl began to cry. She pressed her face against Longarm's chest and sobbed as his arms wrapped protectively around her.

He held her like that for a long time, uncomfortably aware of her trembling body so close against his, and fought against the hard male response that threatened to disclose itself to her.

Damn that Emma, he thought as he held the weeping girl. There was absolutely no comparison between the two of them—the sleek, beautiful madam and this frightened, vulnerable, half-starved serving girl. But damn that Emma for getting him so stirred up.

With an effort of will he pulled away from the girl, tucked her onto the cot Tomlin had so briefly occupied, and covered her with extra blankets.

He kicked off his boots, removed only his vest and shirt, and crawled into a lonely bed. He could still hear the girl crying softly on the other side of the small room.

"Marshal?" Her voice was a barely audible whisper, much too low for it to have wakened him if he had already been asleep.

"Yes?" Tired as he was, he was having difficulty dropping off. He could not quit thinking about Tomlin, about the threat of the Goat Horns, and about that damned Emma. He was achingly hard and erect from thinking about Emma. He could not get the sight of that perfect body out of his thoughts.

"Marshal, I . . . would you mind . . . doing something for me?"

"If I can."

"Would you hold me?"

She sounded frightened. Considering what her life must have been like, from the way he had seen her treated at the cafe and from the look of her back, it would have been impossible for him to guess at the night frights that could plague this thin, drab girl.

"Of course I will," he said aloud. He had a few reservations about his level of control, but he would manage, he was sure.

Her answer was a low rustle of sound as her blankets were pushed back and then the pad of bare feet on the hardwood floor.

Longarm thought of keeping her on top of the covers to remove some of the temptations that were already gnawing deep in his belly in the aftermath of that damned Emma, but down in the basement they had already quit firing the boiler. There was no more heat hissing through the radiator, and already he could feel a chill in the air inside the hotel room.

He felt her at his side and moved over to make room for her. Quickly she slipped under the blankets beside him. He wrapped his arms around her, and gratefully she snuggled against him, her back against his belly and her buttocks pressed close against his crotch. There was no way she could have missed feeling the erection that was pulsing

142

there. He stroked her hair and cheek, trying to soothe and comfort her. She had unpinned her hair, and there was the moisture of tears on her cheeks. The girl continued to press herself against him within the circle of his arms. She sighed.

"What's your name?" he asked. He continued to stroke her, and she wriggled under his touch like a purring kitten. The contact seemed to be exactly what she needed.

"Jenny," she said. "Jenny Foster."

"My name is Custis. Custis Long. But most everyone calls me Longarm."

Jenny Foster began to chuckle and then to laugh at the incongruity of an introduction under such intimate circumstances. They were, after all, in bed together. "Pleased to make your acquaintance, Longarm," she said with mock seriousness.

"And I'm pleased to meet you, Jenny."

She laughed again. The fear seemed to have left her for the time being, and her laughter had a nice sound to it. With another sigh, but a happy one this time, she turned in his arms so they lay face to face and snuggled tight against him.

"Longarm."

"Mmmm?"

"Thanks for telling that man that I'm not no whore. I'm really not, you know."

"I know that, Jenny."

"But I'm not no virgin neither."

"Oh?"

"What I mean is . . . well, you got a powerful need in you. And I wouldn't mind if you wanted me to ease that needing of yours."

"You don't owe me anything, Jenny Foster."

She wriggled a little more and began to kiss his neck

and the hollow of his throat. "It ain't a matter of owing, Longarm. I like you awful well, and I'd be truly proud to be with you, if you wouldn't mind. I mean, I know I ain't anything to look at. And a fine gentleman like you could have any girl that was lucky enough..."

He stopped the flow of words by covering her mouth with his.

It was perfectly true that Jenny Foster was nothing to look at. But there was a sweetness and gentleness about her that the glossy and beautiful Miss Emma could never have hoped to match.

Jenny let out a glad little cry that was muffled by the contact of his mouth with hers and reached between them to fumble at the buttons on his trousers.

Her breath was sweet, he discovered.

She helped him off with the corduroys, then quickly shed her dress and drawers before he could help her.

When she pressed herself against him again her body, thin though it was, was warm and welcoming. Jenny sighed, and her head lolled back against the pillow beside his. Her hands crept between them again to stroke and tantalize him.

He ran the palm of his hand over her nipples and then down across her sunken, fluttering belly. Jenny began to shudder and stiffen after a very few seconds of his manipulations. Abruptly she pressed herself tight against him, trapping his hand where it was while she nuzzled at his neck and clawed his back and buttocks.

Her pleasure came in great, sweeping waves, and she quivered and jerked so violently that if he had not known what was happening he would have thought he was hurting her.

At last she stiffened one last time with a sharp, short little squeal of delight and then went limp, lying almost exhausted at his side with his hand still clamped tight between her upper thighs.

"No good for you, huh?" he asked with a smile.

Jenny laughed and turned her head enough that she could reach his shoulder with her lips. She kissed him there and played the tip of her tongue across his already sensitized flesh.

He gave her time enough to come down from the heights she had just reached, then raised himself over her.

The girl was not exactly reluctant. She kissed the underslope of his jaw and positioned herself on her back with her legs parted to greet him and her arms open to clutch him tight against her.

She shivered with pleasure as Longarm probed for the warm, wet entrance and then lowered himself slowly to fill her. Her arms pulled tighter around him, and she raised her legs to clamp them behind his butt as she urged him deep inside her slender body.

Almost at once he could feel her responses in the tightening of the muscles across her flat stomach and in the convulsive clutch around the base of his shaft.

With a low murmur of contentment, Longarm began to stroke slow and deep inside Jenny Foster.

Chapter 14

Breakfast was grudgingly served and unbelievably expensive, a dollar apiece for a meatless meal of hotcakes and fried potatoes. Longarm was not happy about it, but complaint would have produced nothing but aggravation. He was able to put his own meal on the government's bill, but Jenny Foster's had to come out of his own pocket.

He ate quickly and tossed his napkin onto the soiled plate, then handed the girl the key to his room. "There's something you could do for me today, if you wouldn't mind."

"Anything," she said. He believed she meant it, too.

Perhaps it was only the combination of familiarity and lingering affection, but this morning she did not seem half so drab and homely as she had the day before. Her frail body seemed only pathetic and endearing, and there was a glow in her eyes—quite pretty eyes, he decided—that was nice to see across the breakfast table.

And she had proven her willingness to accommodate not half an hour earlier. He could still feel the delightfully hollow sensation of complete satisfaction south of his belt.

"Someone was in my room yesterday while I was out. They didn't take anything, but I wouldn't want to trust in that luck a second time. Would you mind staying in and keeping an eye on things while I'm out? If I'm not back by the time you get hungry again, go ahead and eat and charge it to the room." The truth was that he did not want her going out again until she had some decently heavy clothing to wear, and he could not take the time now to worry about finding a coat for her.

"Is that all?"

He winked at her. "For now."

The smile that came onto her face was worth much more than the inflated price of the hotel meal.

"You don't mind?" he asked.

"I'd do anything for you, Longarm," she said with simple honesty.

He thought about giving her a kiss when he left, then rejected the idea. Not with others in the restaurant. "I'll be back when I can," he said.

Morning had brought no improvement in the temperature. It was still cold enough to shrivel a buffalo's pecker, but he thought the wind had slackened off some.

The first thing he did when he stepped outside was to check the look of the snow high on the Goat Horns. The awesome, destructive mass still lay there waiting for a victim. That danger had not lessened at all.

Redcloud remained trapped under a soft, white threat.

The townspeople seemed to be adapting to the conditions with the ease of much practice, at least so far as the drifting in the streets was concerned. Men were already out with shovels improving on the paths that had been tramped into the drifts the evening before. None of the stores had opened for business, he saw, although here and there he could see groups of people forming orderly lines in front of one place or another.

In the cold, thin light of the early morning, there was none of the panic that had infested these same men the night before. Longarm took that as a good sign and hurried down the street to the jail.

Evan Maxwell looked and smelled like he had slept in his clothes last night, but he appeared to be sober. If he had had an eye-opener this morning, he had been able to stop at just one. Longarm thought that was a good sign also.

"Good morning, Sheriff." He stamped the snow from his moccasins and closed the door behind him.

"How's it look out there?" Maxwell asked as he fed another lump of soft coal into a stove that was already glowing with heat. It was, in fact, uncomfortably warm inside the dowdy jail.

"Cold," Longarm conceded. "Not so bad as it was, though. The wind is still up, but not like it's been."

Maxwell nodded and clanged the stove door shut.

"How long can something like this last?" Longarm asked.

Maxwell exposed yellow teeth in a grin. "Can? You wanta know how long *can* it last? Shit, man, I'd guess it *can* last till June or thereabouts, though I wouldn't call that real likely."

"All right, then—how long do you think it will last?"

"Now, that's another story, ain't it?" Maxwell pursed his lips and ran a hand over the thick stubble on his chin. He probably had not shaved since the last time he had bathed, and Longarm was distressingly aware inside the overheated room of how long ago that must have been. "The snow's already quit," Maxwell said, "so if I had to guess, I'd say the last of it should be today or tomorrow."

"What about the Goat Horns?"

Maxwell grunted. "That's still another story, Deputy." He shrugged. "That could be weeks. There just ain't any way to tell. Depends on sunshine and temperatures. The difference from night to day, y' see. The faster the snow starts to slump down an' shift, the faster it'll break loose and slide. Won't anybody be leaving outa here nor coming in until that happens."

Longarm hesitated for a moment, then went ahead and asked the question anyway. Poor as Maxwell was as a sheriff nowadays, there were hints now and then that once he had been a reliable man. "Would you have any idea of where I might find Walter Tomlin?"

"What'd you want Walt for?" Maxwell countered.

Longarm felt a moment of discouragement at the thought that Maxwell too might be one of Tomlin's pals.

"Shit, now I remember," Maxwell said with a snap of his fingers. "You come here to make an arrest, didn't you? Walt, was it?"

Longarm nodded.

"You got to excuse my memory, son. I been sick lately."

"Sure."

"He ain't at home?" Maxwell asked. Apparently all knowledge of Tomlin's arrest and escape had escaped Maxwell just as completely as Tomlin—damn well temporarily, Longarm thought—had gotten away from federal custody.

Longarm explained the situation to the now sober and

apparently helpful sheriff. He did not try to spare himself in the telling.

"Now, that's a damn shame," Maxwell said. He shook his head. "Old Walt a thief, huh? Hard to believe."

"I have the warrant if you want to see it," Longarm said.

"Oh, I believe you. Said it was hard. Never said I couldn't do it. Shit, boy, I seen pillars of towns turn to pillars of salt before in my time. Let me tell you I have. Man just never knows what the other fellow's really like. Way I see it, Walt got to like bein' able to set everybody up to everything they wanted an' wasn't willing to quit when it came to be more'n he could handle. I've seen it before, son. I surely have." Maxwell blinked and gave Longarm an owlish look. "Mind if I ask you something, son?" he went on.

"You can ask."

"I seem to've forgot your name, boy."

Longarm laughed and introduced himself again.

"I'll remember this time. I surely will." Maxwell felt through his pockets, failed to find whatever he was looking for there, and looked back at Longarm. "Like I said before, Longarm, nobody's leaving Redcloud for a spell yet. Care to give me a hand with something?"

"If I can."

"I been thinking since I woke up this morning. What I figure to do is t' go around and get some of the leading citizens to stand with me on this plan. A few o' the mine owners, them few as is here instead of laying up with a bunch of French whores in Denver or Sacramento or some-place, and some of the more sensible store owners too. Get them to back me and lay out a plan so no one man can buy more'n so much in a day's time. An' make it clear that if this business with the Goat Horns goes on much longer,

150

we'll have to gather up everything people've already put away and lump it into one storehouse for distribution a bit at a time."

"You've seen something like this before," Longarm observed, thinking about the miner who had been at the cafe table.

"Ayuh, I have, Longarm. Seen weak folks come close to starving when other sons o' bitches were sittin' on more food than they could eat in a year of working hard at it."

"You said you've seen folks come close, not that you've seen any actually starve."

Maxwell grinned and chuckled. "I been carrying a badge a long time, son. Always took it serious, too. Before I got . . . sick, anyhow. No man's gonna starve where Evan T. Maxwell's in charge. Not 'less we *all* starve at the same time."

"That sounds fair."

"That's what the law is all about, boy. Fair." Maxwell nodded emphatically.

"I'll be glad to help any way I can, Sheriff," Longarm said.

"Then let's get out an' around, son. We got a lot of folks to talk to this morning." He reached for his coat.

The wind died late in the afternoon, as suddenly and as completely as if some celestial force had shut a gate on it. People on the street who had been hunched over against the force of it stopped where they were, straightened, and smiled. Then, almost as quickly, they began to look with apprehension toward the Goat Horns and the terrible power that lay high on the mountaintop, locked there only for the moment, waiting to come thundering down without warning. It was as if they all realized that only the destructive force of an avalanche remained as the final phase of the

151

spring storm that had paralyzed their community.

Longarm joined them in looking up toward the Goat Horns. He doubted that he could have avoided that if he had wanted to. The presence of the threat was hypnotic. The valley where Redcloud lay was deep in shadow behind the surrounding wall of mountains, but the prominent Goat Horns were picked out in bold relief by what remained of the late-afternoon sun, hidden far off to the west.

A man standing near Longarm on the street shuddered and crossed himself. His reaction, Longarm knew, had nothing to do with the cold, which continued deep and hard despite the cessation of the wind.

Throughout the day Longarm and Maxwell had been talking with businessmen of the town, singly at first and later in a meeting with all of Redcloud's leading citizens in one room. Longarm was frankly impressed by what the now-sober sheriff had been able to accomplish. Voluntary controls had been placed on the sale of food and of coal. With luck, there would be no more cause for panic among the townspeople.

Now, the meeting over, Longarm was on his way back to the hotel. Maxwell was trudging through the deep snow toward the jail.

"I'll see you later," Maxwell said. He was already forty or fifty yards distant, angling farther up the street toward the jail building. Longarm lifted his arm to wave.

Something plucked at his sleeve, and the pedestrian who had just crossed himself sat down abruptly in the snow.

A moment later there was the report of a gunshot.

Longarm threw himself forward in a rolling dive. He came up with the collar and left sleeve of his coat packed with wet snow but with the Colt in his hand.

Behind him bright blood showed on the thigh of the man who had been unfortunate enough to be standing close

152

by. The man screamed once in pain, then tried to grit his teeth against it.

Longarm scuttled forward into the protection of a snow-drift just in time to evade a second rifle shot.

"On the hillside!" Maxwell yelled. "Behind the whore-houses. Can you see it?"

"No. Wait. Yeah, I can see some movement."

"That's right."

The range was impossibly long for a handgun and probably too long for anything but the most expert rifleman, but Longarm took careful aim and threw a slug toward the ambusher anyway, just to keep the bastard honest.

"That made him jump!" Maxwell shouted.

"I can't see him now."

"I can." Maxwell was farther out in the street and had a slightly better angle of view. "Damn, I wish I hadn't sold my gun."

Longarm refrained from comment, but it was a hell of a thing for a peace officer to sell his weapons, and probably for a bottle of cheap liquor.

"Hot damn, boy," Maxwell cackled with glee. "You got 'im now."

"Where?"

"The silly son of a bitch's cornered himself," Maxwell called. "Can you make out that path where he was?"

"Yeah."

"He's gone up it. Nothing at the end of it but a mine shaft. The silly bastard has put himself in a bottle, and you're the cork, boy."

Longarm grunted and stood upright. There was no sign of the gunman now. He could see nothing up on the mountainside except white snow and gray rock. But if what Maxwell said was true . . .

'D'you want him, boy?"

"Hell, yes, I want him." Eyes still searching the empty ledge where the rifleman had been, Longarm reloaded the empty chamber of the Colt.

"There's a path leading up to that ledge, boy. Go through that alley over there and straight on up."

Longarm nodded. "Holler if he shows himself while I'm behind the buildings."

"Go get 'im, boy. I'll keep an eye on it for you."

Longarm broke into a run. He dashed between the buildings where Maxwell had indicated and found a snow-filled path leading up the steep mountainside toward the ledge where the rifleman had been. Obviously there was more than one way up, because the path had not been used since the snow came.

"Watch your step, damn it!" Maxwell called. The old man's voice sounded thin and distant.

Longarm had to holster the Colt and use both hands to steady himself as he climbed the rocky, snow-packed trail. When he reached the narrow ledge leading across the mountainside, the going was better. Not good, but better. He slowed his pace. He had no more desire to be killed by a slip on the snow and a fall than he did to be shot by some bastard with a rifle.

"You got him now, boy." Maxwell's voice barely reached him on the ledge.

Down below Longarm could see a crowd gathering in the street. Several men were kneeling beside the man who had been accidentally wounded. The rest were watching Longarm and the ledge in front of him.

Footprints showed in the snow on the ledge, a single set of prints. The rifleman had gone up it but had not been able to return. And there would be no way out for him now but directly past the man he had just tried to shoot down.

Longarm moved closer to the mountainside and drew the Colt again.

He moved forward slowly. He could see nothing in front of him but the empty ledge and the footprints leading on ahead of him.

There. A dark hole gaped in the side of the mountain. The footprints led inevitably into it. Longarm pressed himself against the cold rock and inched forward.

The mouth of the shaft had been timbered and a small overhang built to guard against slides of rock and debris from above. There was room enough at the side of the entrance timbers for Longarm to squeeze in there, out of the line of fire from anyone inside the shaft. He leaned against the heavy vertical timbering and held the revolver raised and ready.

"You inside!" he called.

There was no response.

"You can't go anywhere, man. Lay down whatever weapons you've got and come out with your hands behind your head."

It occurred to him to wonder if there was only the one man inside the tunnel or if he might have a partner with him. Just because only one had been spotted did not necessarily mean there were no others.

"Come on out," he called again.

"Come and get me," the rifleman challenged. The voice was muffled and hollow-sounding as it emerged from the mouth of the shaft, but Longarm did not think the speaker was very far inside the tunnel. He had no way to tell, but as far as he knew the tunnel could extend a mile into the mountain.

"Is that you, Walt?"

"Fuck off."

155

Longarm had heard that voice before. He did not think it was Tomlin, but he was sure he had heard the voice.

"You're trapped, man. Give it up before I have to shoot you."

"Come on in, you son of a bitch. I'm ready for you."

I'm sure you are, Longarm thought to himself. Aloud he said, "Last warning."

"Screw you, mister. Just try and take me."

Longarm had no doubt whatsoever that the rifleman was waiting with his aim steady on the mouth of the shaft. The remaining daylight outside the tunnel would silhouette a perfect target against the light if anyone tried to charge the shaft opening.

Longarm had no intention whatsoever of being dumb enough to charge in after the fool rifleman, nor did he have to, not so long as rock remained harder than lead. And, so far as Longarm knew, that physical law had yet to be repealed.

He did not bother to take aim. He did not have to. He held the Colt at the side of the entrance timbers with the muzzle pointed more or less inside the shaft and triggered a round.

From where he stood he could hear the ringing clatter inside as the slug whined and ricocheted deep into the rock-walled shaft.

Longarm pulled back away a bit from the mouth of the shaft and reloaded. "Ready to come out now?"

The answer was a hollow explosion from inside the tunnel as the rifleman fired a useless shot toward the entrance where Longarm stood, protected by countless tons of solid rock.

Shit, Longarm thought. Still, there was nothing he could do about it. He had given all the warnings he intended to give. He damn sure was not going to give the rifleman a free shot at him.

He moved closer to the tunnel mouth again and lifted the Colt. This time he sent four rapid shots into the shaft. The singing, zinging ricochets sounded like a swarm of hornets as they slapped back and forth between the rock walls.

The gunman inside screamed, and Longarm heard a sharp, metallic clatter as a rifle was dropped onto hard rock.

Longarm reloaded the Colt and held it ready for another unaimed volley.

"Help me. Oh, Jesus, help me." The man's voice sounded weak.

"I will," Longarm called, "if you can drag yourself out to where I can see you."

"Help me."

"Get yourself this far and I will."

"I can't. I'm shot too bad."

The kind of man who would ambush another with a rifle had been known to lie before. And Longarm had no desire to make himself meat for a liar playing possum.

"Come out or I'll have to let go again," he called.

There was no answer.

He pointed the Colt into the shaft, careful not to expose himself to the rifleman's fire, and again triggered a fast four shots into the tunnel.

This time the screech of pain was sharper and louder.

"You bastard!" the rifleman shouted.

"Want to come out now?"

"You really did shoot me, you son of a bitch."

"Crawl."

A moment later he could hear faint scuffling noises.

Longarm reloaded and waited patiently for the rifleman to reach the mouth of the tunnel. It took a long five minutes before he could hear the wounded man just inside the mouth of the tunnel.

"Will you help me now, damn it?"

"Throw the rifle out where I can see it."

"I can't. I left it back inside the damn shaft."

"Then crawl the rest of the way out. You already took all the chances I expect to give you." As soon as he was done speaking, Longarm moved as far back against the timbers as he could get and dropped low into a crouch. The sound of his voice had been from a standing position and would have spotted him for the gunman if the idiot wanted to push it any further.

He could hear more scraping and then a muttered curse. He hefted the Colt and held it ready, just in case.

There was a moment of silence. Then a man's figure, upright and moving fast, appeared outside the tunnel as the rifleman threw himself out.

The muzzle of the carbine was aimed about chest level for a man who was standing, but pointed over Longarm's head.

Longarm triggered his shot first, and the .44-40 slug embedded itself in Franklin Jewett's chest. Jewett's finger tightened on the trigger of the old Maynard carbine, and its bullet blew a stinging rain of rock chips out of the mountainside above Longarm's head. He could feel some of the rock splinters rattle onto his Stetson, but that was all.

"Shit," Jewett fussed. He was down on his back. The slug had taken him in the lungs. Bright bubbles frothed the blood that was pouring out of the chest wound. More blood stained his hip and thigh where one of the ricochets must have clipped him.

The Maynard lay on the ledge. Longarm kicked it, and it skittered away to slip over the edge and fall in long, bouncing jumps down toward Redcloud.

Jewett looked up at Longarm. He was pale, his face tight against the pain. "Am I dying?"

"Yes."

"Fucked up, didn't I?"

"Yes," Longarm said again.

The man tried to grin, but his expression twisted into a grimace of pain instead. "That'll . . . teach me . . . won't it."

"You sure do go all out for a friend," Longarm said.

"Shit," Jewett told him. "Figured . . . you'd get around . . . to ringin' me into it . . . too. Sooner or later. Figured . . . I'd get my licks in . . . while I could."

"Like that, huh?"

Jewett nodded and bit back a groan as another wave of pain wracked him.

"You were home free and didn't know it," Longarm said.

"No shit?"

"No shit."

This time Jewett did manage to get a grin out.

"I don't suppose you'd care to tell me where I can find Tomlin?" Longarm asked.

"Go to hell . . . Deputy."

"I might," Longarm agreed, "but you'll damn sure be there before me."

Jewett tried to grin again. He did not have time. In the middle of it his eyes lost their focus, and his head lolled to the side.

The bright spark of life faded from them quickly, and they took on an empty, glazed look.

Longarm shook his head and stood. He looked around.

The crowd was still down there on the street, watching. He could see Maxwell waving to him. He did not feel like waving back. Apart from everything else, now he had to get that son of a bitch Jewett back down the mountainside.

Chapter 15

Longarm was worn out by the time he got back to the hotel, physically drained by the effort of bringing Franklin Jewett's body down and soul-weary from the uselessness of the man's death. It simply had not been necessary. But better Jewett than himself, damn it.

Maxwell had certainly been pleased about it, though. "Thanks, son," the old man had said. "I don't allow that kind of thing in any town of mine, you know." He spoke as if Longarm had done him a favor by taking care of it before Maxwell handled it himself. Just what the old man would have done, and him not so much as owning a firearm any longer, was left unstated. Longarm did not embarrass the old boy by bringing the subject up.

Now, though, he was damn well tired. He stopped in at the hotel restaurant long enough to order a packet of sandwiches and other such truck and carried the food up to the room. He had not eaten since breakfast, and the girl was probably hungry also. He had not had time to think about her during the day, much less see her, since he left her after breakfast, and he did not feel up to climbing the stairs an extra time so he could bring her down to the dining room. He was that tired.

He dragged into the room, to be greeted with a smile and a flurry of glad kisses. Jenny Foster's pleasure at his return was almost enough to make him perk up again.

"You look terrible," she said with concern.

"Thanks." He dropped his hat on the cot and stripped off his coat. Jenny knelt and helped him off with his moccasins.

"You don't have to do that."

"But I want to." Still on her knees, she took his hand and kissed it, then turned it over and kissed his palm, allowing her tongue to roam lightly over it. He felt a stir of interest that he truly had not expected.

"Tired?" she asked.

He nodded, but refrained from explaining. There would have been no point, and he did not particularly want the reminder that an accounting of the tale would require.

"I know just what you need." Before he could question what she had in mind, she jumped to her feet and hurried out into the hall.

Longarm slumped onto the edge of the bed and bit the tip off a cheroot. He lighted the cigar and leaned against the headboard.

Jenny was gone perhaps ten minutes. When she returned she was helping an acne-pocked youngster lug a copper-lined tin bathtub. She quickly disappeared again and helped the kid haul in buckets of steaming hot water until the tub was half full.

The boy set the last empty bucket down on the floor when they were done. "You c'n dip the used water out an'

162

throw it out the window," he said. "Easier'n carrying it all downstairs again."

Longarm thanked him and found a coin for a tip. He knew Jenny would not have any money. It was not a subject that had exactly come up between them, but she would not have been picking rags out of the trash heaps if she had any money.

When the kid was gone and the door had been bolted behind him, Jenny helped Longarm off with his clothes.

She hugged him tightly for a moment and pressed her lips against his sweaty chest, then guided him into the tub.

The hot water engulfed him, the heat of it seeping into tired muscles and washing away more than the sweat or grime that might have been on the outside of his hide. Maybe the girl had been right. Maybe this was what he needed. He jammed the cheroot between his teeth and closed his eyes, enjoying the feel of the heat that surrounded him.

Jenny went to the washbasin the hotel provided and got a sliver of hard soap and a washrag. She came back to his side, rolled up her sleeves, and knelt.

"Lean forward," she said.

"Honest, you don't have to do all this."

She gave him a bright, broad smile. "I already told you. I know that. Now hush up and let me do something for you for a change."

He really did not want to protest any further. Hell, he might convince her to quit. And he didn't want to do that. He closed his eyes again and leaned forward so she could scrub his back.

"Stand up now," she ordered after a bit.

He did as he was told.

"Mmmm." She lathered the washrag and then with great care washed his genitals.

"There is something to be said for this business of being given a bath," Longarm observed.

"Isn't there?" Jenny agreed.

She rinsed him with gentle and thorough attention. By then his apparatus was much easier to handle, because it was standing out where she could get to everything handily.

With a low chuckle, Jenny kissed him there.

"Are you sure you want to start this already?" he asked. "We haven't even eaten yet."

"We can eat later," she said cheerfully. "In fact, we can do this now. And then eat. And then do this again."

Longarm pretended to consider her suggestion. "If you wish," he said with mock seriousness.

"Good." She helped him out of the tub, insisted on toweling him dry, and then led him to the waiting bed.

Longarm was still tired, but not in the same way that he had been. Now it was a pleasant and relaxed tiredness.

"You're good medicine," he said softly.

He dropped the stub of his cheroot into an old sardine can that had been placed on the nightstand for an ashtray and closed his eyes.

Once again he was engulfed by warm, moist sensation, but this particular method of it was much better than the bath had been.

Someone was knocking at the damned door. Longarm blinked and rolled his head so he could see the window. It was barely coming daylight.

Longarm must have been considerably more tired than he had realized the night before, in spite of, or perhaps because of, the bouncy fun and games with Jenny. Instead of coming fully awake, alert and ready for anything, he felt logy and only marginally in contact with the world. His

164

head ached and there was a foul taste in his mouth. Jenny was still sound asleep.

"Just a minute."

He swung his feet off the bed, yawned, and pulled his trousers on. He turned back to make sure Jenny was decently covered, then plucked the Colt out of the holster on the bedpost. He was still a bit foggy, but he wasn't stupid.

"I'm coming."

He stood to the side of the door when he opened it and confronted his visitor with the business end of the .44-40.

"I don't believe it."

He didn't, either.

"Hi." A grinning Walter Tomlin stood there, thumbs hooked in his waistband and a scent of hair tonic, or perhaps something else, surrounding him. He looked fit, well fed, and content with the world.

In fact, he gave every appearance of being pleased to see his old chum Longarm again.

"Mind if I come in?"

"Jesus." It was all Longarm could think of to say, but he stepped back and let Tomlin in.

"I see you've kept my cot for me." Then he saw that the bed was occupied, a spill of long hair fanning out across the pillows. "Oops! Do you want me to come back another time?"

Longarm scowled at him and went to the nightstand to fetch his handcuffs. He leveled the Colt at Tomlin and tossed the cuffs to him.

"Hey, you don't need those." Tomlin grinned. "I'm here, aren't I?"

"Put the cuffs on."

Tomlin shrugged and snapped the steel around his own wrists.

165

"Hands against the wall. Stand out from it and lean into it."

"Whatever you say, Longarm."

"Where the hell have you been, anyway?"

Tomlin's only answer was another of those cheerful grins.

"And why'd you come back?" the deputy went on.

"Hey, ease up, will you? I did come back."

"And I'm asking you why." Longarm moved closer and began to search Tomlin. Not just a quick pat-down, but a thorough inspection of every possible place a man could think to conceal a weapon.

"You don't have to worry about that. Guns aren't my style, friend."

Longarm continued the search anyway. "You haven't answered my question."

Tomlin shrugged. "It's looking bad for the town, Longarm. Could be a helluva long time before the Goat Horns shed and we can get a train in. So I thought I'd volunteer to do something about it." He winked at Longarm. "You'll tell the judge about me giving myself up and saving the town, won't you?"

"I don't know that the town particularly needs saving right now. Things seem to be under control, for the time being, anyway."

"But you'll tell the judge, right?"

"I'll tell the judge," Longarm acknowledged.

Tomlin grinned again. "I knew there was some reason I liked you, Longarm."

"Jewett's being shot wouldn't have anything to do with your decision to come in, would it?"

"Hey. How can you ask me that? Didn't I give you my parole? Huh? And here I am, just like I said I'd be. I just

166

took a little time off for some last-minute play. You know?"

Longarm grunted. It did not particularly signify that he believed Walt Tomlin.

Good old Walt. Good as his word. Bullshit. But there was no point in going into that now.

Longarm looked toward the bed. Jenny was beginning to stir. She would be awake soon. And he remembered distinctly that she was not wearing a nightdress under those covers.

"Turn around, Tomlin."

"Say, you aren't gonna . . ."

"I'm going to put a blindfold on you." He glanced toward Jenny, was was shifting and turning in the bed. The sheet was working its way lower and was close to exposing things that Tomlin had no business seeing.

"Oh. Sure." Tomlin turned his back to the girl and stood patiently while Longarm dug in his carpetbag for a bandanna, which he used to blindfold the man. Then Longarm woke the girl and let her get dressed. Fortunately, she did not seem at all upset about having been found in Longarm's bed. If anything, she was smug about it.

When Jenny was clothed and buttoned again, Longarm removed Tomlin's blindfold and sat him on the side of the cot. He had already seen who Longarm's companion was, after all. There was no sense in trying to pretend it had not happened.

"Would you go down and get us all some breakfast, please, Jenny? Tell them to put it on the room bill."

"Sure." She gave Longarm a kiss and left.

"Now," Longarm said, "what's this business about you coming to the rescue?"

"Just what I said. I thought I'd open up the line so we

167

can get out of here an' so the town can start getting some supplies again. The food stocks aren't all that bad yet, you know, but the coal supply is lower than anybody realizes. I been checking on it." He smiled.

Longarm shook his head. He absolutely did not understand this man. Not in the slightest.

"And you are going to take care of it."

"Sure."

"I don't know, Walt. You just may be the craziest bastard I've ever had to arrest."

Tomlin laughed. He seemed to get a genuine charge out of the comment.

"You really think you can get the rails open again without an avalanche?" Longarm went on.

"Oh, I never said nothing about there not being an avalanche, Longarm. There'll be one, all right. Got to be before we can get those rails open and get out of here. But it'll be *my* avalanche, not the Goat Horns'. And it won't do anything to hurt my trains. I'll see to that." Tomlin was grinning again.

Longarm could do nothing but shake his head. This was absolutely the strangest man he had ever had cuffs on, and that covered a pretty fair amount of territory.

Chapter 16

Tomlin sent word for the railroad crew to assemble at the station, then walked with Longarm to the building. They had to wade through deep snow to reach it. Obviously the building had been unused since the storm ended. But then, Longarm realized, there would have been no need to man it, with the telegraph lines out and the tracks so completely blocked. The interior of the small building had a tomblike chill. With no sunshine able to reach inside for the past few days, the indoor temperature felt far colder than that outdoors, and probably was well below zero.

Walter Tomlin pointed Longarm toward a chair and went about the chore of building a fire in the potbelly stove despite the disadvantage of the handcuffs. He did not bother to ask Longarm to remove them.

The crewmen straggled in over the next forty-five minutes. By then the depot was cheerfully warm again, heat from the roaring stove quickly driving out the deep cold.

Except for seemingly quite normal greetings to his men, Tomlin held off speaking until they were all there.

"Thanks for coming in, boys." He sat perched on the edge of the telegraph desk, making no particular show of the handcuffs on his wrists, but not trying to hide them either. He seemed completely at ease.

"First thing I want to tell you is that you aren't any one of you to think you ought to have some reason to be pissed with Marshal Custis Long here." He nodded toward Longarm.

"It's a natural fact, boys, that I was stealing and that Franklin was in on it with me. Franklin made the mistake of trying to kill the marshal. That was Franklin's decision. Not mine an' not the marshal's. All Longarm done was to keep himself alive, and I expect any one of you would've done the same. So there's no need for any of us to resent Marshal Long over it. You got that?"

He looked each one of them in the eye, his gaze moving slowly about the room, and waited until he had a nod of agreement, however reluctant, from each of them.

"All right." He paused and looked around again. "I've had a good time up here, but I done what they say and now I got to pay the piper. Meantime, it's up to us to take care of this town an' get the road open again. That's what we do, boys, and together we do it better'n anybody I ever seen or heard of. We're gonna do it again." He grinned at them. "The bunch of us together."

The men had been silent up until then. His grin and his talk sparked them. They were genuinely proud of being part of Walt Tomlin's crew, and if he said they were going to do it, why, they were damn sure going to go out and do it, come avalanches, snowdrifts, or hellfire.

"Kent," Tomlin went on, "I want you to go round me up some pipe. Steel pipe off of steam fittings or whatever.

Maybe Mr. Tindell has some at his store. It has to be steel, though. No lead. I need a section six or eight feet long, with an inside diameter of, oh, two inches or thereabouts. Then I want some more pipe sections—steel would be best but lead will do if we have to, no terra-cotta—with an outside diameter just about the same as the inside diameter of the other pipe. I want that smaller stuff in sections about a foot long. Pieces that will fit down into the long pipe. You got that?"

The man called Kent nodded.

"So hop to it. When you have it, carry it down to the shop. The smaller stuff can be in one long piece, Kent. Bill can cut it to size here. Okay?"

Kent nodded again and left.

"Bill, I want you to dig your way inside the shop and get it operating. Soon as Kent gets here with the pipe, I want you to take those small sections and thread them on both ends. Shit, I almost forget. Tony, run catch Kent and tell him I want steel caps for both sizes of pipe. One or two for the large piece and a couple dozen for the smaller size."

"Right." One of the men buttoned his coat and hurried out after Kent.

"Anyway, Bill, I want those small pieces threaded on both ends and holes, like about three thirty-seconds in size, drilled through the caps. And thread one end of the big piece too. Can do?"

Bill gnawed at a twist of chewing tobacco and gave Tomlin a sour look. "Can a goose shit?" Then he smiled.

"Good. Go get the shop open and get a fire going. Bring the pipe and caps back here when everything is ready."

Bill nodded and left.

"Warren."

"Uh-huh?"

"I need you to take some of the boys to help you carry

171

things and start hitting the hardware stores. Round me up a couple drums, call it four hundred feet anyway, of fine cable, a quarter inch or so. Doesn't matter if it's copper or steel just so it ain't too heavy. And let me think. I think maybe some long strips of sheet tin or whatever light metal you can find. Find you some snips and cut it if you have to. Four inches or so wide, you don't have to be real careful about it, and as long as you can manage." He thought for a moment, then nodded, mostly to himself. "Yeah, that should do it."

Longarm was perplexed. What any of this had to do with the shovels and snowshoes he had expected, he could not imagine. Still, Tomlin seemed to know what he wanted, and therefore what he wanted to do with it.

The section chief went on to detail other men to other jobs. He wanted a keg of blasting powder, single F or giant granulation, which certainly would be no problem in a mining town. And a box of fuse cord, slow-burning, not more than a two-inch-per-second burn rate.

He sent someone else to find some woodworking tools. The railroad shop was equipped to handle almost anything dealing with metals, apparently, but had practically no tools suitable for working wood. Then the man was to cut wooden disks, each at least an inch thick, to fit inside the long pipe Kent would be bringing back. Two dozen of those.

And a bucket of grease.

And a brace with some small bits.

And, finally, the snowshoes and sandwiches Longarm had expected him to ask for to begin with.

By the time the last man had been dispatched on the unusual foraging detail, Tomlin seemed completely satisfied with whatever the hell his plan was.

• • •

They were kneeling, just the two of them, in the hole the men had cleared in the snow down to and slightly below ground level. It had taken some hard pick and shovel work to make the base Tomlin wanted, but now they were ready.

Tomlin insisted on performing this last task personally. And Longarm was just as insistent that he remain at Tomlin's side throughout the procedure. He was not about to let Walter Tomlin handle explosives without Longarm being there to watch every move.

Tomlin's plan might actually work, too, Longarm conceded. Damned if it just mightn't.

What the man had done was to build a cannon, and with an explosive shell at that.

The six-foot-long section of large steel pipe Kent had found had been capped at one end with a hole in the cap where a firing fuse could be fitted, then heavily wrapped with copper cable to strengthen the piece of pipe that was about to become a cannon barrel.

A layer of tight-wound cable had been wrapped around the full length of the pipe. Then it was sheathed in roofing tin and wrapped with yet another layer of the tightly wound cable. Theoretically—and this part had yet to be proven— the reinforced steel would be strong enough to contain the explosion of a propellant charge of powder inside it.

The small foot-long sections of pipe were the explosive charges.

"We'll make a bunch of them since we don't have any way to know what to expect for range and accuracy. But with luck the first one will do the job." Tomlin had grinned and added, "I'd rather not fire off this son of a bitch more'n once if I don't have to."

Longarm fervently agreed. There were no guarantees that the homemade device would not blow up the first time they used it. The odds of a mishap would only get worse if

173

they had to shoot repeated charges.

The explosive charges were made by capping one end of the short pipe pieces, each of which was a slip fit into the "bore" of the homemade cannon, and then filling the pipe with powder. The other end was capped, and a five-second fuse was fitted into it.

To keep the projectile from blowing up as soon as the cannon was fired, the fuse end was then slipped through a hole in one of the wooden blocks Tomlin had had made, and the edges of the wood wadding was thickly coated with grease, to keep flame from the propellant charge from reaching the projectile end of the fuse and prematurely exploding the shell.

Tomlin dumped about a pint of Single F powder into the muzzle of the cannon, then fitted the greased block with a tip of fuse exposed to the cannon charge. The idea was that the firing of the cannon would light the fuse, which would then burn while the shell was in flight and detonate the shell far up toward the Goat Horns. He followed it with the makeshift shell. He used a broom handle from the depot to ram the shell down to the base of the smooth-bore cannon, then got to his knees and fitted the firing fuse into the cap at the base of the cannon.

"What d'you think?" he asked. He sounded pleased with himself.

"I think it's a hell of an idea. If it works."

"Me too."

The reinforced-pipe "barrel" was resting on a low wall of sandbags, pointing at roughly a forty-degree angle into the air and aimed in the general direction of the Goat Horns. More sandbags had been laid on top of the barrel to keep the recoil of the propellant explosion from bouncing the cannon too wildly out of line.

"All we got to do is get the explosion close enough and loud enough to set off the avalanche," Tomlin said. "We don't have to hit anything in particular. Just make a big enough bang that it'll start the slide. After that, Longarm, we're in business."

"It could work."

Tomlin grinned at him. "Want to light 'er off?"

"It's your baby. You do the honors."

Tomlin nodded and bent over the base of the cannon, which was resting in a small pocket gouged out of the hard earth to handle the expected recoil.

"Here goes nothin'." Tomlin scraped a match aflame and held it to the tip of a twenty-second length of fusecord. The treated cord sputtered and began to emit a thin stream of smoke as the controlled burn took hold.

"Let's get the hell out of here."

Longarm agreed. The two men galloped awkwardly through the deep snow to a point sixty or seventy yards off, where the rest of the men were waiting.

They reached the others and turned, out of breath and puffing, to wait for the explosion.

There was nothing.

They waited.

Nothing.

"Shit," somebody said.

"She fizzled."

"Slow cord," someone else suggested.

"Well, I damn sure ain't going over there to see."

Longarm turned toward Tomlin. Just then he heard a dull, hollow report, not nearly as loud as he would have expected. When he looked back toward Tomlin's home-made cannon he could see only a few sandbags where the gun had been.

"Did it blow up?"

"Naw, it just flopped over backward."

"But the shell went. I seen it go."

"You're outa your mind, asshole," someone else protested. "You couldn't of seen it."

"I did, I tell you."

"Wait!" Tomlin hushed them in a sharp voice. He was counting slowly under his breath. "Four. Five." He frowned. "Aw, hell. Six. Seven."

Half a mile or more toward the Goat Horns and still in the air there was a quick flash of yellow flame, followed moments later by the sound of the explosion. Men began to yell and to clap Tomlin on the back.

"She works. The son of a bitch actually works. Your shell went off."

"Wait." Tomlin was still concentrating on the twin crags of the Goat Horns.

The explosion had been close, but had it been close enough? Or loud enough?

For long seconds there was nothing. Then, very slowly at first, even from this distance they could see a faint, fluid shifting in the enormously deep and heavy pack of snow that lay up there.

It was as if the snowpack were rearranging itself.

Then, gathering speed and power with the irresistible force of a train, but magnified a thousandfold or more, the snow began to flow.

Behind them Longarm could hear the glad shouting of the townspeople of Redcloud as they rushed outside to watch the Goat Horns give up their threat.

Moments later and he could not have heard if someone had fired Walter Tomlin's cannon again.

The avalanche began slowly but within seconds was a

wall fifty, a hundred feet high of loose, moving snow, each foot of fall gathering more snow and more weight before it until the avalanche was beyond any power Longarm had ever conceived.

The sound of it reached him then, a low-pitched moan that built quickly into a roar.

Even from this distance he could feel a wall of cold wind against his face and chest as the avalanche displaced the still air and kicked it rudely out of its path.

"Jesus," Longarm whispered.

The avalanche roared down into the narrow canyon, sweeping trees and house-sized boulders before it like so many wisps of lint, and raced on, curling up the other side of the canyon wall like an ocean wave, curling at the top and falling back into the canyon floor, dragging with it still more tons of snow and rock and splintered vegetation.

A stormcloud of loose snow drifted and swirled on the crazily dancing air, filling the canyon until there was no more visibility possible, until it looked like the entire gap between the mountains was a blind white mass.

"Lordy," someone said in a reverent voice.

Longarm realized only then that it was the first sound he had been able to distinguish since the roar of the avalanche had begun.

The sound of the fall had been so great that he had been able to feel it more than hear it. It had been beyond the ability of mere ears to register.

Longarm shuddered. No wonder the people of Redcloud had been so nervous. If anyone had been caught in that . . . Longarm shuddered again. There would be nothing left for anyone to find and bury. Nothing at all.

As the thrown snow began to settle out of the air he could see that the shape of the canyon appeared to have been changed. It was impossible to tell how deeply the railroad tracks were buried now. Thirty feet? Possibly more.

Even so, now the trainmen would be able to cope with it. However deep it now was, they would be able to dig out, make whatever repairs they had to, and eventually get a train through.

Whatever was required, Tomlin's crew would accomplish it. It might take days or even weeks, but they would get the job done, and when they did there would be no danger now of an avalanche crushing the men or destroying their work.

He shuddered one last time as he remembered the awful force of the avalanche, then turned in time to see Walter Tomlin walking toward a tool bag one of the men had left in the snow.

Tomlin looked at Longarm and winked. "A snort of brandy sounds good about now," he said cheerfully. He bent over and reached inside the bag.

Chapter 17

It was no flask or flagon Tomlin pulled from the bag. His expression hardened as he straightened to an upright position with a sawed-off stub of shotgun in his manacled hands.

Longarm could see the weapon with total clarity despite the twenty or twenty-five yards that separated them.

It was a single-barrel shotgun. An old one, muzzle-loaded and percussion cap fired. It had been sawed short at the barrel, leaving only eight or so inches there, and the stock had been cut down as well so that only a pistol grip remained.

Tomlin cocked the shotgun and pointed it at Longarm's torso. He was no longer the grinning, friendly fellow who had turned himself in that morning.

"No choice, Longarm," he explained. "I couldn't spend all that time behind bars."

"You're being foolish, Walt," Longarm said, deliberately using the man's given name for the first time since Tomlin had returned.

Tomlin shook his head. He looked determined. Behind Longarm the crew members had begun to notice. They were shifting quickly out of the way of Tomlin's fire. "Who d'you think can stop me once you're gone, Longarm? Maxwell? The old fart doesn't even own a gun. No, I'll go down and tell the boys in Silverton what needs to be done. Somebody has to do that anyway. First thing after you arrested me, Franklin sent a no-traffic order down the line an' then jimmied the wires. Somebody's got to tell them to come ahead with the rescue crew. I'll do that, and then I'll go off to someplace where nobody's ever heard of Walt Tomlin." He smiled, although a bit sadly. "Someplace warm, I think. Your people will look for me, but they won't find me."

"That isn't what I meant, Tomlin. You're being foolish. Now lay the gun down and come along nice and easy."

"I can't do it, Longarm. I just can't."

"You'd better. I don't know what else you have in that bag, Walt. I'll kill you for sure if you open up on me."

Tomlin raised an eyebrow and brandished the short-barreled shotgun toward the lean deputy.

"It won't work, Walt."

Longarm wanted to explain. He genuinely intended to. Tomlin did not give him time.

The man raised the stubby shotgun, still pointing it at Longarm's torso, and pulled the trigger.

Longarm's right hand flashed under his coat. He palmed the Colt and fired as a stunned, gaping-jawed Walter Tomlin stared at him.

The slug took Tomlin in the chest and sent him to his knees. The man was tough and determined. Longarm had to give him credit for that. He propped himself up with one

180

hand and groped inside the tool bag, probably looking for another weapon or some way to reload the shotgun.

Longarm shot him again, and he flipped over into the snow.

"Shit," Longarm said. He looked around to make sure no one else wanted to take part in Tomlin's play, then began to reload the Colt.

He fidgeted and brushed at the front of his coat occasionally as he did so.

For days, damn it, he was going to be picking shot out of that coat. And it was the best one he owned. He hoped Tomlin had not done too much damage to it.

He reached inside it and fingered the lining until he found and extracted one of the pellets that had lodged in the sheepskin. Number six shot, he judged. Certainly no heavier than number five. He shook his head.

"Told him he was being foolish," he muttered to no one in particular.

A muzzle-loaded shotgun had little enough power to begin with. With the charge coming out of a pistol-length barrel its power was little more than that of an India-rubber slingshot. At a distance of five yards, Tomlin could have blown Longarm in two. At ten yards the weapon would damn sure have killed. At twenty-five yards the birdshot was a minor annoyance, and even buckshot would have held little real danger.

"Foolish," Longarm said again.

He looked around toward the train crew, the Colt still in his hand. None of them seemed interested in looking him in the eye.

There likely was no chance he would ever find out who had left the shotgun in the bag for Tomlin to use. Hell, it might have been none of them.

Tomlin obviously had made his arrangements before he

181

showed up at Longarm's hotel room that morning. He could have paid anyone to do it, including Miss Emma or any of her girls. That narrowed the list of suspects to just about every man and woman in Redcloud. That was more than Longarm wanted to bother sifting through.

He looked down the valley toward the snow-filled canyon. A white mist of blowing snow still affected the visibility there. He still could not believe the power of that avalanche.

"Whichever one of you is in charge now had better get a snowshoe team organized and send them down to Silverton," Longarm said. "You heard what Tomlin told me. They won't be sending a train up until you get word to them."

The stationmaster bobbed his head and turned nervously toward what was now his crew. The men paid him little attention, though. They kept looking over toward Tomlin's lifeless body and at the red stain that was beginning to congeal in the snow under him.

Longarm shoved the Colt back into its holster and looked down the canyon again.

Not that there was much point in that. Probably not for days.

Maxwell would still have to regulate the use of food and fuel until the tracks were reopened. Longarm would have to help him with that, probably.

And there was no way to notify Billy Vail of what had taken place in Redcloud until the tracks were reopened.

Tomlin had said Jewett deliberately cut the wires to the telegraph, but that would have been of interest only yesterday. No telegraph pole could have withstood the force of the avalanche off the Goat Horns.

So they were still well and truly isolated until the railroad crews working from this end and from Silverton could meet somewhere in the canyon and reopen the tracks.

Longarm glanced back toward the hotel.

He would be stuck here for some time, but . . . there might be certain compensations.

Jenny Foster was still up there waiting for him.

One thing sure, he thought. He was going to have to have that snippy desk clerk take the extra cot out of his room. The bastard was still putting it on the government's bill, and Marshal Vail would sure fly off the handle at that.

Longarm turned and headed back toward the hotel.

Not until he was a hundred yards or more away did the men of Walter Tomlin's crew begin to drift over to the side of their former boss, to pick him up and tend to him and probably to grieve for him too.

Longarm, though, felt no grief whatsoever for smiling, friendly, finally murderous, good old Walt.

Watch for

LONGARM ON THE SIWASH TRAIL

ninety-third novel in the bold
LONGARM series from Jove

coming in September!

54

JAKE LOGAN